The Rules

for the Game of Life

The Rules
for the Game of Life

An inner dialog,
in which *secrets are revealed*.

Allen Cobb

Mulberry Knoll
Fairfield, IA USA

Printed in the United States of America. No part of this publication may be reproduced, stored in a retrieval system, or transmitted in any form or by any means, electronic, mechanical, photocopying, recording, or otherwise, without prior written permission of the publisher.

First printing 2013

ISBN-10: 0-9792104-2-9
ISBN-13: 978-0-9792104-2-6

Library of Congress Cataloging-in-Publication Data:

The opening quote is from Jammer, Max, *Einstein and Religion: Physics and Theology*, Princeton University Press. The quote is reproduced in other sources, with some inconsistency in the two bracketed words. The intended words as shown should be perfectly clear from the context.

Mulberry Knoll
www.MulberryKnoll.com

To Mary

Your laughter will echo forever in my heart.

We are in the position of a little child entering a huge library filled with books in many languages. The child knows someone must have written those books. It does not know [who]. It does not understand the languages in which they are written. The child dimly suspects a mysterious order in the arrangement of the books but doesn't know what it is. That, it seems to me, is the attitude of even the most intelligent human being toward God. We see the universe marvelously arranged and obeying certain laws but only dimly understand these laws. Our limited minds [cannot] grasp the mysterious force that moves the constellations.

Albert Einstein, (c. 1929)

Contents

Prologue

One of Harvey's earliest memories was sitting in a huge armchair that was big enough to hold at least half a dozen more Harveys between its huge soft arms. He was propped up in one corner of this vast padded platform, and someone was tapping his lower lip with one finger. It felt very good. Then someone began tapping his chin, and that felt nice, too, but then they stopped. He looked up and there were some people standing around, mom and dad and others, huge people towering high above the huge armchair. The people's heads were very far away, but they were smiling.

One day he noticed that some of the sounds he heard were coming out of people's mouths. Later, of course, he would understand it as talking, but at first it was just a jumble. Sometimes mom would move her mouth and high exciting sounds would come out. Dad's sounds were rougher and deeper, but not as loud.

Days or months later, sitting again in the huge chair, he laughed out loud. Lights were flying around the room and he couldn't stop watching them. There was a ringing sound in the room. Mom and dad were somewhere else; he could hear them talking far away. The ringing felt good inside, and made him laugh some more.

Then another sound appeared, like mom's and dad's, but closer. It was so close he twisted around in his blanket and tried to see where it was coming from. The new sound was just little blobs of noise, like pretty much everything, but he liked it, so he giggled and waved his arms.

Harvey had another early memory, in which lights were floating around over his crib. Maybe it was just one light of many colors. He heard the ringing tones again, and knew they sounded like bells. There was more talking, just one person very close, but there was nobody in the room. He knew they were words, but he didn't really understand them. Or at least the memory didn't include any content.

As an adult, these memories became lost, but he did recall them a few times when he was about twelve years old. One time he was sitting with his parents in front of the big fireplace. There were several feet of snow outside, and they were all safe in the house with plenty of food and firewood. He closed his eyes, and then remembered the huge armchair, and he also remembered the voice, when nobody was in his room.

He looked at his parents and wondered if they could remember anything from when they were infants. Most people said it wasn't possible, but most people also said that most people don't know anything. Harvey's inner dialog had begun; life was about to get complicated.

He pondered these tenuous memories that drifted in from the very beginning of life, and then his attention shifted to the big white pine alongside the side lawn. It was overloaded with snow, and even the sturdy lower branches bent close to the ground. The winter sun was glinting off ice crystals and playing tricks with his eyes.

. . .

Over the next few years, his parents died, one after the other, of natural causes. Harvey was surprised that the grief depicted on TV barely entered his awareness. The funerals were sad affairs, and ironic, since neither parent had wanted one, but the sadness came from the guests, not from his own heart. Maybe he couldn't feel grief, or perhaps it was so intense he repressed it, or maybe he hadn't loved his parents enough. Lack of grief spawned increased guilt. Things were getting complicated.

He went to college, in part to discover why people went to college. The answer eluded him, but he had a good time and learned as much as people usually do in their late teens. College prepared him for preparing, but not for a career. Afterwards, he spent a year visiting friends, now scattered around the country. Then he moved back into the big house in upstate New York, which was now his sister's, hoping to find work for the summer. Work didn't materialize, but he did rediscover the white pine by the side yard.

The tree was where he had learned to climb, and he still loved to watch the woods from its sprawling branches, and it turned out to be a landmark in Harvey's life.

Ω

Chapter 1

Game

Harvey was 24 years old and he was sitting on a lower branch in the tall pine tree overlooking the lawn next to his parents' house. They were no longer alive and Harvey's sister and brother-in-law lived there now; Harvey was just visiting.

As he sat on the tree branch, he noticed a sudden glimmer, shimmering, as if the sun were reflecting off something metallic out at the very end of the branch. It was a stout enough branch to sit on, but not strong enough to crawl very far from the trunk, so Harvey just sat there, staring, and tried to figure out what was glinting.

Something metallic definitely seemed to be catching the light of the sun. As he stared at it, the glinting turned into a glare, and he suddenly realized his entire visual field was consumed with brightness. Not sunlight, per se, not the kind of light that would make you squint, but an unfamiliar rich glare that seemed to bloom inside his head rather than on his retinas.

And then a voice spoke to him. And the voice said, "Harvey. Behold the game of life. Welcome."

Harvey looked around. There was no one there. And then he realized the voice was inside his head. A moment later, he remembered that this was a classic symptom of early onset schizophrenia, and he thought, *Uh-oh. I could be going crazy.*

The voice immediately spoke again, inside his head, and said, "No, Harvey, you're not going crazy. And no, this is not you speaking to yourself. And no, this is not a hallucination. This is the voice of God."

At this point Harvey knew that either he *was* crazy, or God was nothing like anything he might have expected — talking inside his head, in this blunt, uninspiring fashion. Though he had to admit the bright light had evoked a vague sense of profundity.

I wonder if I'm supposed to speak out loud to reply, he thought.

"No," said the voice. "Speaking isn't necessary. Surely you've read enough science fiction by now to know that."

"OK," thought Harvey, somehow directing his mental verbalizations toward what might be the origin of the voice, albeit inside his head with everything else. "But how do I know you're actually God?"

"Everybody worries about that," said the voice. "In fact, it isn't all that important to know who I am."

"But what if I've gone crazy?" Harvey said. "I can't just take your word for it. And I can't even tell if I'm talking to myself, either."

"It must be exasperating."

"Well, damn it, it is." Harvey suddenly realized he had said 'damn.' What if it really was God? Had he just been swearing at God?

"That's not swearing," said the voice. "And of course I heard it. I've heard every thought you've ever had."

Oh Jesus, thought Harvey. *That's absolutely the most horrifying idea I've ever heard of—God hearing all my thoughts. All those ... inexcusable ... repugnant ... regrettable ... thoughts. Oh shit, I just said 'Jesus.' Oh no, I said 'shit.'* His head was spinning.

"Look," said the voice. "I'm not here to blow your mind. The whole point of speaking to you is so you don't have to spend your life worrying."

"Worrying?" said Harvey, wondering what the difference was between his usual inner dialog and the present one.

"About me," said the voice. "Among other things, you don't need to worry about me hearing your every thought. I hear everyone's every thought, and believe me, this stuff is not something anyone would pay much attention to. It's just like the wind blowing in the trees. You hear it, but you don't try to pick out the sound of each individual leaf."

Harvey's mind was busy mulling, without directing any thoughts intentionally at God, or whoever it was.

"Besides," continued the voice, "your reaction to your own unwanted thoughts is reason enough to be forgiven for them. I know what your highest aspirations are."

The wind had picked up, and the big branch Harvey was sitting on bent and shivered. A sporadic hiss surrounded him as the breeze moved through the canopy of pine boughs. He tried to imagine hearing the fine fibrillation of just one pine needle.

"Shall we get back to it?" said the voice.

"My highest aspirations?" he asked. "Because I haven't a clue."

"Guess again."

"Back to the game?" Harvey asked.

"Yes, that."

"OK. So you're going to tell me how I'm supposed to be playing this so-called game of life?"

"Nothing much about how to play it," said the voice. "But I thought you should know the first rule."

"OK," said Harvey again. "Do I need to know the rules? Does everybody know these rules?"

"Good grief no, Harvey," the voice replied. "Hardly anyone knows *any* of the rules."

The voice fell silent, and then continued. "Well, perhaps some people figure out a few, but most people are pretty much in the dark." Then it said, brightly, "But I've chosen to explain them to you."

That's nice, thought Harvey, and then realized he might as well have said it aloud.

"And I'm giving you Rule 1 now, to prime the pump," the voice continued. "As you grow older, when the time is ripe, I'll hit you with another rule."

"You know," said Harvey, "You really don't sound a lot like God."

"I realize that," said the voice, "since I'm almighty and all-knowing. But for the same reasons, I couldn't care less what I sound like."

"OK," said Harvey, for the third time. "What's this rule I'm supposed to know?"

"Oh, it's nothing much. It's just ***thou shalt play the game***."

"That's it?"

"Yup. That's it. Couldn't be simpler."

"So basically you're just saying that I have to play."

"That's right."

"But I don't know what I'm supposed to do."

"That's right."

"Well then, how am I supposed to play?"

"Just play, and you'll find out." The voice paused and then said quietly, "You might consider that finding out is part of the game."

"Oh, so it's an empirical game. I play, and then something happens, and then I find out I just broke a rule."

"Something like that," said the voice. "But I wouldn't worry about it."

"Maybe *you* wouldn't. But then why bother telling me the rule?"

"Because it's good to know."

"What difference does it make, if there's no alternative anyway?"

"It always makes a difference, knowing a little more. Knowledge is always useful, sooner or later."

"What happens if I don't play the game?"

"You'll get bored."

"You mean the whole point is just to keep me from getting bored?"

"Yup, that's pretty much it," said the voice.

"I don't see why that's so important that God has to come and tell me in person."

"Well, it'll become a lot more obvious later on."

"So the only punishment for breaking the rules is boredom?"

"No, no, that's not a punishment. That's a consequence."

"So if I break a rule I get bored?"

"No, if you break *this* rule you get bored. And then the boredom turns into depression. And the depression, if you're not careful, becomes an addiction from which you might never escape."

"Ah. So you're warning me against falling into a trap."

"Yes, you could say that. I guess it could be helpful that way."

"OK," said Harvey. "I'll try to avoid the trap. Hell, I don't mind playing the game. I guess I must have been playing it all along anyway, haven't I?"

"You sure have."

Harvey thought a moment. "Then even with the rule, there's really no difference at all, is there?"

"The only difference is that now you know."

"Now I know what?"

"Now you know you have to play."

"Well, OK, sure. But I still don't have a clue what use to make of this. The rule — or the game, for that matter."

"There's no need to make anything of it. Like I said, it's just good for you to know. The rest will become clearer after you've spent some more time in the game."

Harvey scrunched around on the tree branch. The light in his head had gone away. Maybe it was just a special effect the voice used to make the experience more memorable. No, that was ridiculous. Having conversations with strangers inside your head is memorable enough.

Then he realized, or sensed somehow, that the voice was gone. "Hey," he said, inside.

Silence.

The wind was getting chilly; it was early fall. Harvey climbed down out of the tree and walked back to the house. His sister and brother-in-law would be home from work soon, and he didn't want them to know how much time he spent in a tree. He was 24; it was time to get serious.

Ω

Chapter 2

Rules

The weekend came, and there were people around all the time, so Harvey didn't get back to the pine tree for a while. It rained all day Monday, and Tuesday he had to get his decrepit car to the garage and back, but Wednesday afternoon was open, and he went to the tree at his first opportunity and climbed to the highest fat branch, about ten feet up.

"OK," he said, or announced, to himself.

Silence.

"Well, I'm here again, finally," he said. "Whenever you're ready."

Sitting in the tree had been a favorite pastime for much of Harvey's short life, so it was only natural to lean back against the trunk and gaze through the branches at the blue sky, and let his mind wander.

After an hour or so, a voice said, "No flashing lights this time, eh?"

Harvey jumped, and grabbed onto a nearby branch. "Is that you?" he said.

"Who else?"

"Well, I don't know," Harvey began.

"You hear lots of other voices in your head?" said the voice.

"Well, no, but..."

"Never mind. It's me. No problem. Same old same old."

"Are you going to tell me some more rules?" asked Harvey.

"Yessir. One more. That's what I'm here for," said the voice.

"Well, I'm ready. I can't say I got much from the last one, but at least I know where to get the next rule."

"The last one was the first one," said the voice.

"Huh?"

"The last rule you got was the first rule on the list," said the voice. "I thought that was an interesting conceptual twist."

"Oh."

"The second rule begins like the first one, with a 'Thou shalt'."

"That's nice, I guess. What is it?"

"***Thou shalt not necessarily be told the rules***," said the voice.

"That's it?"

"Yup."

"Wow."

"Wow that's amazing, or wow ironically?"

Harvey tried not to respond, but his head immediately filled with scattered phrases, many of which weren't very polite in the presence of God, if indeed that was really who the voice was.

"I see," said the voice. "Ironical wow."

"Well, jeez," said Harvey, whining mentally. "Rule 2 is that you aren't told the rules? What kind of rule is that?"

"It's a pretty important one."

"But you're telling me the rules right now! It's a contradiction! It doesn't make any sense."

"Of course it does. The rule is that you won't necessarily be told the rules. It's a perfectly good rule; one of my favorites."

"But you're *telling* me the rules right now, so it's just wrong."

"What about 'necessarily'?" said the voice.

Harvey groaned inwardly. "Oh," he said. "So you *might* not have told me any. But you did. So I guess I'm an exception, is that it?"

"Well," said the voice, "look at it this way. If I hadn't told you these two rules, then Rule 2 would be correct — you might be told the rules, or you might not."

"Yes, but..."

"And you're not the only person in the world I'm telling them to."

"Oh, well, I..."

"Did you think you were? Sorry about that."

"No, I..."

"Actually, I tell lots of these rules to tens of thousands of people. Millions, actually. So you're not an exception."

"I had no idea."

"Did you think you were the exception? The exception that proves the rule, so to speak?" Inside Harvey's head the voice laughed quietly at its own joke, if it was laughter. Actually, it sounded more like bells. Harvey tried to mentally stifle a mental groan.

"But what's the point of making that a rule?" asked Harvey.

"For one thing, it let's you know that you might not be told all, or even some, of the rules. But more importantly, it tells you that other people might never be told any rules at all."

"But rules do apply to everyone, right?"

"I thought that was obvious. In fact it's so obvious, it's not even a rule."

"It wasn't that obvious to me," said Harvey.

"Why do you think I called it the game of life?"

Harvey didn't have an answer. Eventually he said, "I guess I didn't take it literally."

"Well, you should take everything I say literally. You know who I am."

"Actually, I don't know. You could be anyone, really."

"Do you know anyone else who can talk inside your head?"

"No, but that doesn't prove you're God. That should be obvious, even if you're not God."

"Good point," said the voice. "Like I said, it's utterly unimportant for you to believe I'm God."

"Well, to be perfectly honest, I don't," said Harvey. "Not yet, anyway." *Better safe than sorry*, he thought, more or less to himself.

"No problem. You've got the first two rules, and that's what counts. Doesn't really matter where you get them."

"Well, it does make a difference when you hear them spoken inside your own head," Harvey objected.

"True enough," said the voice. "But some people see them written on the subway walls."

"Really?"

"Yup. And a lot of other ways, too. Look, this voice in the head thing, it only works for certain kinds of people. If I could just talk directly like this to most people, believe me, that's what I'd do."

"But you can't? Even if you're God?"

"Good point, Harvey. But that's correct: even God can't force people to understand anything."

"Why on earth not? What's the point of being God? I thought you were omnipotent."

"I am. And there's no point — being God isn't something that has a point. And I can't, because I put people here to learn, not to be told. Much less to be forced."

"Then why are you telling me?"

"Because I don't have to use force."

"Is that a good thing or a bad thing?"

"That's entirely up to you."

Ω

Chapter 3

Options

It was a couple of weeks before Harvey heard the voice again. He visited the tree as often as possible, without prompting remarks on lifestyle choices from his older sibling, but the voice wasn't happening.

Then, on Hallowe'en night, Harvey was alone in the house, for a change, and decided to put on his down coat and go try the tree again. He had barely climbed up to the fat branch when there was a little sound like a screw-top soda bottle opening, probably in his mind, and the voice said, "Happy Hallowe'en."

"You pay attention to old pagan holidays?" Harvey said.

"Not really," said the voice. "But I'm aware of what's going on. That should be obvious."

"You don't mind if they're pagan, I assume."

"They're all pagan as far as I'm concerned," said the voice. "Assuming that by 'pagan' you actually meant 'heretical.'"

"Well, I wasn't really thinking about it. Isn't Hallowe'en a pagan holiday?"

"Depends on your point of view, obviously," said the voice.

"Well, it's from an old, dead religion, isn't it?"

"Nearly all religions are old and dead, aren't they?"

"Wow," said Harvey. "That's cold, coming from you." He paused. "Assuming you are who you say."

"You're never going to let that go, are you?" said the voice. "But tell me what you think makes a religion *not* old and dead."

"Obviously if it's recently created it's not old," said Harvey, with a touch of irritation. "But dead? The ancient Roman gods aren't around anymore, are they? The religions of ancient Greece or Egypt are all gone now. So they're dead. But Christianity, Islam, Judaism, Hinduism, Shinto …"

"Are you sure?" the voice interrupted, producing a first for Harvey: his own thoughts interrupted by his own thoughts. *Another sign of madness?* he wondered.

"Sure of what?" he said. "Mormonism isn't an old religion is it?"

"Nope, not historically, but the values and ideas are as old as civilization. Same with all the others."

"OK, from that point of view, but …"

The voice interrupted again. "Something wrong with that point of view?"

"Well, I mean …"

"Isn't the whole point of a religion its values and ideas? Rather than the year it was invented?"

"Of course, but …"

"Then, from where I sit, they are pretty much all the same. They all want to guide people to the highest good, the greatest fulfillment, the fundamental truth, and so on."

Harvey didn't speak. He was trying to quickly summarize everything he had learned in 24 years about all the great religions of the world. It wasn't much, but it was hard to summarize. He began to feel like he was taking a pop quiz in 8th grade civics class.

"Are you saying that all religions are after the same thing?" Harvey ventured.

"Yup. Pretty much."

"But the religions themselves wouldn't agree at all!" Harvey had glimpsed a chink in the voice's argument.

"Who wouldn't agree?" said the voice.

"The religions. The head honchos of the religions. The elders, high priests, popes, or whatever."

"Oh, you mean the heads wouldn't agree. But the heads are just people."

"Some religions think the heads are in direct contact with you on a regular basis."

"Ah. Those are the prophets. Yes, real prophets sometimes get direct input from me," said the voice. Then it said, in a kind of mental whisper, "Like you are, right now, by the way."

Harvey wobbled on his tree branch. *Am I a prophet?* he thought, to himself.

"No, no, no," said the voice. "You're not a prophet. Not everybody who has contact with me is automatically a prophet. You're not a prophet until you start prophesying. Please don't start that anytime soon."

"I won't," said Harvey, with some relief. A relative silence emerged in Harvey's mind, but it didn't last.

"I forgot where we were going," said Harvey.

"Yes."

"What were we talking about?"

"Does it matter?" said the voice.

"I think it was important," said Harvey. "We were on some big philosophical thing."

"Hallowe'en?" said the voice.

"Oh! No, not Hallowe'en, but you said all religions were old and dead. Then you said their concepts were old even if the religion itself was new. But you didn't say why you think they're all dead."

"Good work, Harvey!" said the voice. Harvey wondered if it had a slightly sarcastic tone.

"I'm not being sarcastic," said the voice. "I never do that. Too dangerous."

"What's dangerous about sarcasm?" asked Harvey.

"When you're God?" replied the voice.

Harvey leaned back against the pine tree trunk. "Oh," he said. *That could lead to all sorts of horrendous mistakes,* he thought.

"It sure does," said the voice, pensively.

"Then tell me what makes a religion dead, if it isn't old and abandoned."

"What's the basic purpose of a religion?" the voice asked.

"To guide people towards moral behavior?"

"That's one, but it's not basic enough."

"To teach people to worship you?" Harvey said, uneasily.

"What's the point of doing that?"

"Well, don't you like being worshipped?"

"What possible effect could worship have on me? I'm already omnipotent and omniscient. I'm already all love, and all good, and the basis of my entire creation. Worship? It's nice, sure, but hardly of much significance to me."

"Yes, but isn't worship good for the worshipper?"

"Yes, exactly. It's something the religion gets the members to do, and the reason for doing it isn't for me at all. It's just good to put your attention on me."

"OK, although I don't quite see how that works."

"I'll explain later," said the voice. "But in any case, worship isn't the fundamental purpose of religion. Keep guessing."

This is a bit silly, thought Harvey. Then he said, "To relieve people's fear of the unknown?"

"Good one!" said the voice. "That's a favorite for the atheists. 'Religion is created to provide comfort.' All that trouble and all those complexities, and people fighting to the death — just to provide comfort."

Harvey had nothing to add, but the voice did. "People can be amazingly dense," it said.

"Religious people or atheists?" Harvey asked.

"All of them," said the voice.

Harvey sat on the branch in relative silence, thoughts flitting around like a cloud of gnats, but nothing directed at the voice, and nothing worth writing down.

An owl hooted softly in the dark woods. "I give up," Harvey said.

"The basic purpose of religion is to make people happy," said the voice.

"That's it? Just to make them happy?"

"Yup. That's where it all starts, and then every religion gets more and more complicated until there's no sign of the original purpose at all, and the essence of the thing is dead."

"But religions are usually against all kinds of things that make people happy," Harvey protested. "They ban things, prohibit things, punish people for partying, and all that stuff."

"That's because they've decided that real happiness is deeper than getting drunk or just having a good time."

"Then why condemn having a good time?"

"Because they decided it interferes with the deeper happiness."

"But the Romans had gods that were specifically for getting drunk and partying."

"Different people, different time, different gods," said the voice.

"But surely it's not all arbitrary."

"It's not. The basic goal is happiness, of the best kind, whatever that is."

"Well, then what is it? The best kind of happiness?"

"It depends on what you believe in, what your values are, what you like and dislike."

"But that's always different for different people, and different civilizations."

"Yup. It sure the heck is."

He didn't say 'sure the hell is'! thought Harvey, and then wished he hadn't.

"OK," said the voice. "It sure the hell is."

Harvey tried not to respond. He furrowed his brow and stared out into the night. "If religion is basically trying to provide the best kind of happiness," Harvey finally said, concentrating, "then why doesn't it work better? People in any religion have plenty of unhappiness, and I'm sure there are also lots of happy atheists."

"Precisely," said the voice.

"I don't get it. You just said the best happiness depends on who you are, what you believe."

"Yes, and religions are trying to provide one kind of best happiness for all the people."

"Go on."

"It should be obvious. No one kind of happiness is going to work for all kinds of people."

"But why is that? Aren't there some kinds of happiness that work for everybody?"

"Sadly, no. Remember, deep happiness depends on what you believe, and on your values. Some people have a lot to learn, while others are pretty wise. Some are very young, like yourself, and others are living in a war zone, fighting to survive hour by hour."

"So you're saying that religions can't make people happy. But they certainly try to provide the best advice for getting to the deepest kind of happiness."

"Right you are. They try, and it helps. But no organization can possibly get it right for all its members, in all situations, in all ages. So the main purpose ends up failing, everywhere, all the time."

"That's a pretty heavy indictment of religion," said Harvey, amazed that God, if this was God, would even think such a thing. Even if he was just thinking aloud inside Harvey's head.

"No it's not," said the voice. "I applaud the best efforts of religions, when they're not lost in doctrine, politics, and power grabs. I applaud above all the saints and seers and prophets of all the religions, because they're talking from experience."

"OK, then you're actually not down on religion, per se."

"Heavens no! That would be a terrible state of affairs. What a concept! God hates religion!" There was a giddy musical noise in Harvey's head for a few moments. *Is that God laughing?* he wondered.

"Chuckling," said the voice. "When I actually laugh, stand back."

Harvey could only guess what full-blown laughter from God might be like, but he wasn't sure it would be a good thing to experience up close.

"Don't worry," said the voice. "I would never do that inside your head."

That's a relief, thought Harvey, mostly to himself.

"So the 3rd rule should be pretty obvious now, yes?" said the voice.

"Um, not really."

"Rule 3 is my favorite: ***To enjoy is optional.*** Short and sweet."

"Really?"

"You always say that when you hear a new rule."

"It's so glib. I mean, enjoyment can't just be a simple choice. Life's too complicated. Things happen."

"Yes, but whenever you ask yourself if you're happy, you have that choice."

"Not when a tiger is chasing me through the forest!"

"You've been chased by tigers recently?"

"No, but how can you be happy when you stub your toe, or get dumped by your girlfriend, or get the flu, or fail your French final?"

"It depends on what you believe in, and what your values are. So it's all a matter of where you put your attention."

"But what could make me happy about getting dumped?"

"You have to choose which thoughts to pursue. You can think about getting dumped, or you can look deeper and see how you actually feel about yourself. Yourself, not your dumpedness."

"Isn't that just forcing a Pollyanna kind of attitude? Everything is just fine, even if I'm miserable?"

"Well, it's not actually a bad thing to pretend you're happy. Even just using your facial muscles to make a happy face will change your biochemistry — I made it that way!"

"You're serious? Making a face?"

"Yes, but my point isn't about faking anything. I'm talking about choosing where to look."

"You mean I can choose to look at pictures of my ex-girlfriend or at pictures of Lake Tahoe?"

"Sure. That would work. But remember, the real purpose of religion is to provide a way to the deepest happiness. Even the happiness of being with your girlfriend is not as deep as knowing who you really are."

"I don't even know what that means: who I really am. I'm Harvey. That's all I know for sure."

"Inside this Harvey you think you know, somewhere around here..." the voice paused, and Harvey felt a warm familiar glow expand deep inside, near his heart, "... there's something more than a name."

"Well, yes..."

"And down there you know perfectly well that you're fundamentally happy."

"Kind of..."

"And if you can even just glance at that place, even when your girlfriend dumps you, you'll see that at least there you're still happy."

"I guess..."

"That's the choice. That's why to enjoy is optional."

"I see," said Harvey. "I guess." But the warm spot was still glowing, and the October breeze didn't feel chilly anymore.

And the voice was gone.

Ω

Chapter 4

Everything

Harvey met an old friend from college who was visiting family in a nearby town. His friend spotted Harvey in a brightly lit gourmet supermarket. They went next door to a tavern and had a beer and talked about life after college. Harvey's friend was making a lot of money now, and had a new BMW, which he had driven cross-country from California. Harvey was impressed. When his friend asked what Harvey was up to these days, a deep gloom came over him, and he couldn't think of anything to say. He wasn't up to anything, actually. His life was a random meandering.

Harvey's friend was very understanding, so much so that by the time Harvey returned to his sister's house he was too angry and depressed to speak civilly when his brother-in-law asked him to join them for dinner. He muttered something unintelligible about taking a walk, and stomped, as quietly as possible, out of the house.

After a few minutes wandering old familiar paths through the nearby woods, he ended up at the pine tree. He looked up at the branch where he usually sat, and wondered if he could even begin to converse with the voice. It was too humiliating to be so angry while knowing it was for no good reason. His friend hadn't been condescending — just a little too understanding.

He shouldn't have come to the tree. He wasn't ready for conversations with anyone, much less disembodied voices claiming to be God.

"Hey," said the voice. "Come on up." It sounded cheerful and relaxed, which immediately made Harvey even more resentful.

"What do you mean 'up'?" Harvey said. "You're in my head, not up in the tree."

"Well, both, actually," said the voice. "But you look like you could use a little cheering up."

"Not from God, thanks," muttered Harvey, absently noting that it was apparently possible to mutter a thought.

"You can whisper a thought, too," said the voice. "Or not think anything at all."

Harvey said nothing to the voice, but his head was slowly examining a jumble of anger and disappointment, which made him feel worse.

The voice was silent.

Harvey leaned against the tree and jammed his hands in his pockets. The breeze of coming winter had a brisk edginess that reminded him of standing alone outside the house in the city, waiting for the school bus, with his bookbag and a ball of fear in his stomach.

The branches rustled softly, and Harvey suddenly turned and climbed up to the fat branch. Thankfully, the voice remained silent.

After a while, Harvey said, "I can't take it anymore."

"Take what?" said the voice, an obvious question.

"It. I don't know. Everything." Harvey rolled his eyes, physically and mentally.

"The game?"

"What game?"

"Of life."

"The game of … oh. Yeah, sure. It. Everything. The game." He paused. "It sucks," he said. Then he regretted it, started to think up a retraction, then thought an apology was probably better, and then realized he wasn't sure what he was apologizing for, and then it was too late anyway.

"It's OK," said the voice.

"Gaaa!" said Harvey, wishing the voice would go away, and also wishing it would say something helpful.

"What's bugging you?" said the voice, in a whisper.

"You don't already know?"

"Of course I do. But do you? That's what's relevant."

"Yeah—It's my life. I'm not getting anywhere. I have no idea what to do. I've got no future. My relatives think I'm lazy, my friends are all making money and buying cars, and I don't even have a job offer to flip burgers."

"Then raise your sights a little."

"At what? I have no skills. I got my degree in 'liberal arts,' for crying out loud. What good is that?"

"You could teach..."

"Right."

"What's wrong with teaching?"

"Nothing, but I don't have the faintest desire to teach. Besides, I'd just be hanging with more clods like me. The blind leading the blind."

"Then you have to find out what you really want to do."

Harvey blanched. He had already tried to figure out what he wanted in life, a hundred times, and gotten nowhere.

"There's no way I can do that! It's impossible. I have no skills for that..."

"Sure you do. You've got twenty-four years of experience, tons of book-learning, thousands of human interactions, good family, good health, and a lot of other assets."

"What good is all that? It's just layers of stuff. It doesn't tell me what I want — in fact, it makes it harder!"

"Well, this seems like a good time to let you in on the 4th rule."

"Oh, great. Will this help me decide?"

"You're not in a position to decide."

"What? I thought that was exactly what you said I have to do."

"You can't decide until you have something to decide about. You haven't even identified any alternatives, other than flipping burgers."

"OK, so tell me Rule 4." Harvey leaned back against the tree, waiting for something that he knew would make him even more frustrated.

"There's no need to be fatalistic," said the voice.

"I wish you'd stop doing that," Harvey moaned.

"Can't help it," said the voice. "But anyway, Rule 4 is a compound rule, with what you might call two sides to it. ***You've been given everything you need, not more than you can take.***"

Harvey thought about it. There was something *non sequitur* in the wording. "I'm not sure I understand," he said.

"Probably you don't," said the voice. "These things aren't just simple statements of the obvious, you know. Not much point numbering the obvious ones, is there?"

"You're saying I have enough skills and experience to be able to figure out what I should do — is that it?"

"That's the first part. But the second part is more timely, given your present mood."

"I should be able to take it?"

"Take what?" said the voice.

"You know! This stupid situation I'm in, not knowing what I should do, not finding a good job, getting criticized all the time."

"Yes, I'm fully aware of your situation, Harvey. But that's not what you're complaining about."

"Yes it is."

"Is not."

Is this what God is really like? I can't believe it, Harvey thought, supposedly to himself. The voice, apparently, ignored it.

"I'll bite," Harvey said. "What am I complaining about, if it's not all this … uh … *stuff* … I have to put up with these days."

"That was a close call, wasn't it?" said the voice.

"What was?"

"Stuff."

"Oh. Yeah. Sorry. But if the *stuff* isn't the problem, what is?"

"What makes all this *stuff* so important to you?"

"I don't know! That's just the problem. It's so irrelevant, but everybody makes such a big thing out of it."

"Everybody?"

"Everybody who knows me. It makes me feel like ... terrible."

"Ah. Now we're finally getting down to the nitty-gritty."

"What's that?" Harvey was getting more irritated, and more confused.

"Makes you feel terrible," said the voice.

"Yes, it does," said Harvey.

"Well, there's the crux of the matter."

"How I feel? What's so important about that? I can't help it if people make me miserable."

"How soon they forget," said the voice, very quietly.

"Forget what?"

"Rule 3."

Harvey had to think, which wasn't easy at the moment. "Oh," he finally said. "To enjoy is optional."

"Right."

"But wanting to feel good doesn't *make* me feel good!"

"Then don't *try* to feel good. Just remember that it's an option."

"What's this have to do with Rule 4?"

"You haven't been given more than you can take."

"You said that."

"But you didn't think about it. You complained, but you didn't look at the rule."

Harvey thought. *Judgmental people make me angry. But I can take it.* It was true enough — it wasn't unbearable: just miserable.

"Good," said the voice. "And ..."

"And?"

"Rule 3."

"I should just grin and bear it?"

"No need to grin. No need to bear it, either."

"How can I not? I have to deal with it!"

"Do you?"

"Well, I …"

"You just identified the problem: you feel miserable."

"Right …"

"And you know you can take it."

"Right …"

"So put your attention on something other than how miserable you feel."

"OK … I'll try …"

"Seriously, Harvey. Stop trying. Just look the other way for a second." There was a slight tinge of annoyance in the voice. It didn't sound like something he wanted to mess with.

"How many times have you sat up here on this branch?" the voice asked.

"I don't know. Hundreds?"

"How did you feel then?"

"Which time? Last time?"

"Any time. All of them."

"I guess I felt fine. Most of the time."

"Why don't you feel fine now?"

"Well, obviously because I've been thinking about these stupid attitudes everybody has."

"No, it's because you've been thinking about feeling miserable."

"Well I can't help that!" Harvey cried in exasperation.

"You can't help having the feeling, but you can help thinking about it." The voice paused, perhaps letting the words sink in. "You're prolonging the feeling by dwelling on it. Surely that's not terribly difficult to comprehend, is it?"

Harvey suddenly felt really stupid. That made his miserable feeling increase, not decrease. Then he realized he was examining just exactly how miserable his misery had become. And it was true — he really didn't have to do that.

"Great!" said the voice. "So we're done."

"Huh?"

"You've got the message, *finally.* Took a little extra oomph this time, but you got it. I knew you could, because you've been given everything you need. And this stupid situation you're in isn't more than you can take. So you can now at least entertain Rule 3. That's what's so important about Rule 4."

"I'm confused again."

"No you're not," said the voice.

Ω

Chapter 5

Fault

The next day Harvey felt a little better, but then his in-laws started asking him when he was going to move out, and he got even more frustrated and depressed than before. Maybe it was better to go straight to the tree.

He climbed up and sat down, staring angrily through the spikey pine needles at the grey autumn sky. It looked like rain, but rain might turn into snow, and Harvey was definitely not ready for snow.

"Back so soon?" said the voice.

"Not a good time?" Harvey asked.

"Any time's a good time. What's on your mind?"

"As if you didn't know."

"You said that last time," said the voice. "It's getting old. I'm just making conversation to put you at ease. There's no need to be fussy."

"Sorry." Harvey settled back against the rough bark and tried to get comfortable. Usually this perch high up in the tree was good for an hour or more before his back got tired and his butt longed for a cushion.

"Exercising your Rule 3 option a little?" asked the voice.

"Well, I tried, but then they started bugging me about moving out of the house. Christ, I have no place to move to! What do they expect?"

"They want their privacy back."

"Yeah, right. They've got the whole bloody house."

"And they don't think it's their job to build you a life."

"Well of course not. But they don't have to put it all on me."

"Where else should they put it?"

"I don't know. It's just not fair. It's not my fault I'm floundering — things just haven't worked out yet."

"Rule 5," said the voice.

"Oh God." *Oops, sorry, I know, OK, never mind.*

"Rule 5. Ready?"

"I suppose."

"Look, I'm not doing this for my health."

"Obviously not."

"Then at least pretend you're interested. These rules will be helpful now and then, and you'll be glad you knew about them. Take my word for it."

"How could I not?"

"You're becoming so sarcastic it's tiresome. Or would be if I could be tired."

"Sorry. I'll shut up. What's today's rule?"

"Rule 5 is *It's not their fault.*"

"That's awfully specific. My family could at least show some understanding, couldn't they?"

"Not your family. Them. All of them. The whole world. It's not their fault."

"The world? I wasn't blaming the whole world!"

"The point is, it's not anybody's fault."

Harvey didn't answer.

After a minute, Harvey said, "Well, OK, it's not their fault I'm freeloading. I have to admit that."

The voice didn't answer.

"So I guess it's my fault. I should have gotten a job by now."

"I just said it's not anybody's fault," said the voice.

"But it *is* my fault that I haven't figured out what to do yet. I should have gotten it together two years ago."

"Why is it so important to blame someone?"

"Obviously if it's not anybody else's fault, it must be mine."

"The only mistake you're making is that you're spending all your time looking for someone to blame, you or anybody else, instead of putting your attention on what you want."

"But I don't *know* what I want!"

"How will you ever find out?"

"I don't know!"

"Have you tried looking?"

"Of course I have."

"Where have you looked?"

"Everywhere. I've been to job fairs, I took placement surveys in college, I've talked to friends who are already into their careers, and nothing rings a bell."

"But that's all outside."

"What?"

"You're looking outside to find out what you want!" The voice sounded like that was truly a comical thing to do. Faint musical tones floated around the tree.

"Where else am I going to look? I don't have career postings in my head."

"So you're going to look at all possible careers, jobs, lifestyles, until you find the one that rings a bell? That could take a very long time. There are tens of thousands of careers, and another few million things that wouldn't be called careers."

"I know. That's what makes it so damned hard."

"Why ever would you look at a career posting to find out what you want? Isn't that something you have to find inside?"

Harvey stopped waving his arms, mentally, and thought about it. It did make sense. This voice usually did, after you got past its weird way of making a point.

"How do I look for something like that inside?" he asked.

"By not looking."

"Oh boy," Harvey said, and then made a conscious effort not to be cynical.

"Thanks," said the voice. "I appreciate that. Looking inside is something you do all the time. Are you hungry? Happy? Tired?" The voice paused, and Harvey immediately found himself looking around inside to see what might be going on. It was so familiar that he almost couldn't tell he was doing it.

The voice continued. "I can't tell you how to do something you're already an expert at. But if there's something you want to know, and you know it's inside, just put your attention on what it is."

"How is that going to get me an answer?"

"You don't get answers that way," said the voice. "You get direction."

"Direction?"

"A new sense of direction, yes. Later on. And that's what gets the whole system primed, sensitized, for whatever it is you need. So when it comes along, outside, you'll recognize it."

"I don't understand."

"You say you don't know what you want. But in fact, *knowing what you want* is what you want. So you do know what you want."

"Huh?"

"What you want right now is to know what it is that you want."

"That doesn't really make any sense."

"It's the language," said the voice. "Sometimes the language just mangles the meaning. Not everything can be said clearly, even if it's very simple."

"Are you saying that all I have to do is look inside and the answer will eventually pop up?"

"That could happen. But usually what happens is that you look inside, and that sets the stage, and then at some point something comes along *outside* and you find that whatever was puzzling you has been taken care of."

"That could take a long time, like you said."

"It's out of your hands, Harvey. That part of it."

"But that just makes me feel helpless!"

"Sorry. Rule 3."

"But you don't have to make it that way!"

"Rule 5. 'Their fault' includes me, too. It's not my fault. No fault no foul."

"That's not fair! And don't say 'nobody said life was fair.'"

"I won't. That old saw is a cheat. It avoids all the specifics. Life is unfair in several different ways, but fairness is relative. What's fair to you might not be fair to your sister, and vice versa. That's where I come in."

"How so?"

"I make it fair on a grander scale. But we're getting off the track. Since it's nobody's fault that you have feelings of misery, and since you don't have to dwell on that, now you can look inside and get your question clear."

"My question is pretty vague: 'I wish I knew what I need to know next.'"

"That's not vague. It just makes a clumsy sentence. Don't worry about verbalizing it. In fact, forget all about using words, and just know that you need something. And know that you've been given everything you need."

"It's as if all you're saying is 'don't worry, everything will be OK.'"

"That's a fair summary. But it skirts the mechanics of getting things to be OK."

"I guess so. I'm beginning to see how the rules work together."

"Very good. I knew you would."

"Sorry about 'Christ' a few minutes ago, by the way."

"Not a problem. He wouldn't mind, and neither do I."

Ω

Chapter 6

Two

It was a month or more before Harvey got back to the pine tree. He had avoided driving up the long steep road to the old house because of the snow, but now an indian summer was in effect and it felt like spring. His sister and brother-in-law were away on a trip, and the sun was out.

He parked alongside the house, and crunched across the gravel to the woods. The tree was right where he left it. The voice was, too.

"I have to move," Harvey said.

"Where are you going?" said the voice.

"To California. I got a job."

"Congratulations. Have a nice trip."

"I'm not moving right now. In a couple of weeks or so."

"That's nice. Have a good trip in a couple of weeks or so."

"What I meant is," said Harvey, "that I won't be coming to the tree anymore."

"I thought we covered this."

"That it's not the tree? Yes, I realize that. But ever since then, you've only spoken to me when I'm in this tree. It's nice, and I've always loved climbing trees, but the point is I won't be near any trees that I can climb. And I may not have time to be climbing them anyway."

"That's OK. I don't have a special thing about trees."

"So where will I find you? In California?"

"I'm inside your head, Harvey," said the voice, just a little testily. "What are you really asking?"

"I'm trying to plan ahead," Harvey replied. "Should I go to a park? Or will you stop talking to me?"

"Why would I do that?"

"Please stop messing around; it's an important question!"

"Sorry. Just kidding. You should kid around more. You can kid around with me any time, you know."

"I'm trying to be serious," said Harvey, and he realized he was gripping the tree branch with all his might. *I must be really afraid of losing contact,* he thought.

"That's pretty clear," said the voice. "Being serious isn't such a great thing to do. Better to be clear-minded. Seriousness gets your brain all clenched up."

Harvey gritted his teeth, then noticed what he was doing and consciously un-gritted them. He took a few breaths, and then said, "Will I still be able to contact you?"

"You always have been," said the voice. "But I've been contacting you. And I have no intention of stopping just because you're in California."

"Good," said Harvey. "Thanks."

"You're welcome. California really isn't that far."

"Maybe not for you, but for me it's my life savings for a plane ticket and a stack of UPS boxes. And it's nowhere near this pine tree."

"You'd be surprised," said the voice.

"I doubt it," Harvey said. "But I guess I didn't want to lose contact. There are a lot of unanswered questions."

"Yes, aren't there?" agreed the voice.

"So how do I contact you?" Harvey asked.

"You needn't. Like I said, I'll do the contacting. I'm never available except when I'm available."

"That's helpful."

"I have a lot on my plate," said the voice. "In fact, everything."

"I can imagine," said Harvey, sarcastically.

"Sure," said the voice.

"Then what do I do when I'm in California? Should I make a special time? Or what?"

"I'll find you when I have a chance," said the voice.

"When you have a chance?" said Harvey. "If you're God, you can make the chance."

"I can't make you listen," said the voice. "We've been over that."

Harvey sighed and said, "So I'll just wait for you to get in touch."

"Good grief no! Don't wait for anything. Just go on."

Harvey fell silent, figuratively speaking.

"Samuel Beckett said that," said the voice.

"Said what?"

"'Just go on.' But Sam wasn't a happy camper. He had a tough row to hoe, although he did a magnificent job of plumbing its depths."

Harvey hadn't read any Beckett.

"I'm allowed to do that," the voice added.

"Do what?"

"Mix metaphors."

Harvey hadn't noticed any metaphors either.

"On your trip," said the voice, "there's one thing you should remember."

"What's that?"

"Rule 6. ***There are only two players.***"

"Really? Just you and me, you mean?"

"Yup. 6 is an easy one, don't you think?"

"But what about all the other people?"

"What about them?"

"Don't you have to take care of them, too?"

"Sure, except that I don't really have much to do, to take care of them. This stuff pretty much runs itself. Very well designed, if I do say so myself. Intelligence built into everything."

"But still, there are billions of other people out there."

"Oh, to be sure, and billions of ants and termites, right under this tree. And billions of galaxies, with billions of stars in each one, so sure, it's a big project, and it takes all my time." The voice paused, and then added, "But since I made time, that's not a problem."

"Fine," said Harvey. The voice seemed a little too boastful to be God, a little too proud of itself.

"If I didn't love my own creation," said the voice, "why would I bother creating it?"

"I honestly don't know," said Harvey. This was getting ridiculous.

"True, you don't," said the voice. "But you will. Sort of."

Harvey squirmed on his branch. "If there are only two players, doesn't that mean all the other billions of people—and yes, the bazillions more on all the other planets—aren't playing the game?"

"They're playing their own games, just like you."

"You mean there's more than one game?"

"Yup. One per person. And some people get more than one, if you can believe it. Some of them are incredible."

"Then Rule 6 doesn't really mean anything at all, does it?"

"Does too. It means that it's just you and me, kiddo."

"And billions of others."

"Nope. The game you're in is just we two. The fact that I'm in all the games doesn't concern you. Well, it may make you think you're concerned, but it's irrelevant."

"So that means I get your full attention? Doesn't that spread your attention awfully thin?"

"My attention doesn't spread. It permeates."

Harvey mulled it over. Rule 6 was simple, all right, but the implications weren't.

"That's why you don't have to worry about contacting me," the voice continued. "I'll be there. We'll have another talk whenever you're ready."

Harvey sat on the branch, more and more random thought-gnats crowding into his head.

"Whenever I can get a word in edge-wise, that is," said the voice.

Harvey stared out through the branches into the chilly dusk. Winter was back in the air. The long pine needles were vibrating in the light breeze, and his branch was bent down, leaving a large gap in the foliage. The sky was a very light blue, with tiny cloud puffs, and the voice was gone for the day.

Ω

Chapter 6b

One

Harvey got to California without incident, although the getting was itself very much an incident. So much so that within weeks of his arrival he had completely forgotten about the voice, and the rules, and pine trees.

Harvey soon found himself working for one of ten thousand high-tech companies that had sprung up in the late 1970s all over California. He rented a small house in the wilder portion of Malibu, and took some pride in not turning into his personal stereotype of a Los Angelino. This meant that he didn't buy a BMW of any vintage, he didn't join a wine-tasting club, he didn't drink lattes, he didn't care about The Industry, and he still enjoyed frozen pizza.

Then a decade passed by, during which Harvey rose to a position of some responsibility in the company, met the love of his life, and got married. He became firmly rooted in the three Prime Directives of Malibu living: when the five-to-ten-year year monsoon arrives, pack up your valuables and get out; when the seven-to-twelve-year wildfire approaches, pack up your valuables and get out; when the ground starts shaking and bouncing, just ignore it.

He repeatedly observed the homes of his friends and neighbors either slide down a mud-slick canyon or burn to the ground. A few of his friends' homes were consumed at a more stately pace by hoards of implacable termites. Apparently, the entire southern California region floats on an ocean of termites.

These events gradually turned Harvey's attention back to basics. He was shocked to discover so much time had gone by without his having had anything to do with it.

He was driving up the Pacific Coast Highway past Zuma Beach one Friday afternoon, when suddenly he realized that he couldn't remember anything since the McClure Tunnel in Santa Monica. Twenty miles of driving without any awareness of what he was doing was so shocking that he immediately pulled over.

His next thought was that he also couldn't *really* remember anything happening since moving to California more than a decade ago. He was getting towards forty, and it seemed as if half his life had just disappeared. The shock of this second realization was even worse than driving in a daze.

And it was then, while semi-paralyzed by this double-whammy brain spasm, that the voice spoke to him again.

"Yo, dude, what's up?" said the voice.

Harvey was already speechless, so he just stared across the highway at the ocean and concentrated on breathing.

"Yo," said the voice. "You don't have to breathe. Your body breathes all by itself."

I'm not taking anything for granted just for the moment, thought Harvey.

"Well, hey, I thought I'd take this opportunity to check in," said the voice. "It's been a long time, dude."

Harvey frowned with an expertise he could never have achieved as a twenty-four-year-old. "Why are you calling me 'dude'?"

"We're in SoCal. Why else?"

"Nobody actually talks like that around here," Harvey said.

"Nobody in your circle, maybe," said the voice. "But believe me, plenty of people still do."

"Well please stop. It sounds very weird coming from you. And I don't talk or think that way myself, so it's not funny."

"Sorry. I thought you'd be glad to talk."

"Well, frankly, I'd completely forgotten about your, um, visits," Harvey said.

"Correct. But this is such a perfect opportunity I couldn't resist," said the voice.

"Opportunity?"

"It's the first time your mind has been open in ten years, if you must know."

"I was just thinking about that," Harvey admitted. "I can't remember doing anything since I moved from New York."

"You didn't," said the voice.

"Didn't what?"

"Didn't do anything. That's why you can't remember doing it."

"That makes no sense at all."

"You can remember the history of what happened, can't you?"

Harvey considered for a moment. "Yes, I know where I live, what I do for a living. I don't have amnesia."

"So the only thing you can't remember is actually *doing* all the bazillion things that got you to this point in time, right?"

"Yeah, I guess so."

"That's because you didn't do them. That's what I'm trying to tell you. It was supposed to be reassuring."

"Well it's not, because of course I did these things. I rented a house, I bought a car, I got the shipping department reorganized, I got promoted. I should remember doing those things, shouldn't I? Not just the fact that I did them."

"But you didn't."

Now that he thought about it, Harvey realized that this was the way the voice always talked to him, like there was all this basic stuff that only the voice knew about.

"Of course I did. What you're saying is crazy."

"If you did all these things, then why don't you remember doing them?"

"That's exactly my problem. My memory's playing tricks on me. I don't remember driving up the PCH just now, either."

"You've got it all backwards, Harvey," said the voice.

"What are you talking about?"

"You're assuming that because all these things happened, not remembering them means something's wrong with your memory."

"Right."

"There's a big difference between something happening and actually doing something."

"Up until five minutes ago, I was driving this car, and now I don't remember a thing about driving it. It's that simple."

"It's evidence that you weren't actually driving it, is what that is."

"That's ridiculous."

"Paradoxical, perhaps, but not ridiculous," said the voice. "How do you know who was driving the car?"

"Because I'm here, and it's my car, and I'm on my way home on a Friday, and there's no bloody other person in the car!"

"Maybe you just don't remember because your mind was elsewhere."

"Well, yes. Something like that."

"If your mind was elsewhere, what was it doing?"

"I don't know. Thinking about something, planning dinner, anything."

"And who was doing the thinking?"

"Well, I was, obviously."

"What about the driving?"

Harvey paused. "You're saying I'm not capable of thinking and driving at the same time?"

"Pretty much, yes."

"But people think and drive all the time. And they put on makeup, make phone calls, listen to the radio, check the rear-view mirror, and a hundred other things. While driving."

"Not in your case."

"What are you saying?"

"I'm saying that you were so involved in your thoughts that you weren't paying any attention to driving. Is that such a big deal?"

"It is if I drive into a concrete wall."

"Did I say *nobody* was driving the car?"

"You said I wasn't paying attention!"

"No, I said you *were* paying attention. Just not to the driving. But something was doing the driving, even if you weren't participating."

"You mean my body was driving without my mind? Like on autopilot?"

"Yup. You've already established that your mind wasn't driving, so it must have been your body driving, without your mind. What else could it have been?"

Harvey thought about it. There wasn't much to disagree with.

"But why didn't I drive off the road?" Harvey asked.

"Because I saved you," said the voice.

"You what?"

"I saved you. Or at least, my creation saved you. Your body doesn't need much of your attention to do things, especially things it's been doing repeatedly for years. It really does have an autopilot."

"I've never heard of that. Usually when someone loses track of driving they go right off the road and kill themselves, or someone else."

"But you've lost track of a whole decade or so, and you didn't go off the road at all."

"That's just forgetting. That doesn't mean I wasn't doing all those things."

"It's not forgetting. You already said you remember all the things you did. There's nothing wrong with your memory. Give yourself a break."

"But I don't remember *doing* them — that's memory."

"No it's not. You're guessing that you should remember something other than the story of your life, but that's not how memory works. You don't re-experience memories, you watch them, like little movies in your head."

"That's completely off the wall."

"No it's not. Memories are just bits and pieces of experience that have stuck in your brain. They're no more real than facts. And they're a lot less reliable."

"But that doesn't explain why I didn't crash my car."

"I told you. It's because your body doesn't need as much help as you think."

"You mean I could go on driving home, right now, and not pay any attention at all to what I'm doing? That's preposterous."

"OK, then let's just say you were lucky."

"That's not an explanation."

"True. But it gets us closer to one."

"How so?"

"By bringing us to the next rule," said the voice. "Rule 6b."

Harvey thought for a moment. "I don't remember what Rule 6a was. In fact I don't remember any rules with a part A and a part B."

"Rule 6 is 'There are only two players.' I never mentioned it was part A."

"I remember: the game itself really involves just you and me. Because you're God. Assuming you *are* God, which is a bit of a stretch, frankly."

"That's it. Keep assuming, at least for the time being."

"What about all the other people?"

"What other people?"

"You're kidding, right?"

"Yes. Couldn't help it. Sorry." Pause. "Still, like I said last time, the other people are their own responsibility, and for each of them, it's still entirely between each individual and myself."

"So I'm driving the car, and I get distracted, and my body goes on and does everything right, because you're taking care of things behind the scenes. Is that it?"

"No, that's not it. If I went around telling people things like that, they'd all go off the road. Of course a lot of them do anyway, even when I'm trying to help."

"Then obviously I'm completely missing your point."

"You're not driving the car, but your body is, and you're paying attention for a while. Then, without any intent, your attention gracefully moves farther and farther from the body, but the body keeps going on with less and less help from your attention. It never gets to zero. You were never *completely* disconnected from what the body was doing."

"That's splitting hairs."

"Maybe, but you survived, so these particular hairs are worth splitting. Just because you didn't appreciate your connection to the body doesn't mean there wasn't one. Your body does most of the work, most of the time."

The voice waited while the familiar old cloud of gnats buzzed around Harvey's brainpan for a while.

"This routine stuff your body does," said the voice, "It's really not very interesting. Why would you remember it?"

Harvey's brain still buzzed with incomplete thoughts.

"If you were drunk, or falling asleep," the voice continued, "then the connection would break. You'd go off the road, and, depending on various factors, end up in a wreck."

Harvey thought some more, and wished he didn't have to think so much.

"That's my whole point," said the voice. "You don't have to think so much. Hardly at all, in fact."

"OK," said Harvey, feeling more defeated than enlightened. "Let's say you're right. Let's say I was somehow still giving the body a tiny bit of attention so it could drive while I did some thinking."

"Go on."

"And let's say that the last thirteen years I've been doing the same thing with my whole life, letting my attention wander around with nothing but a tiny thread back to all the things I'm doing throughout the day."

"You're definitely getting warmer."

"Great. But that means I'm just barely getting by. It's a wonder that I've achieved anything at all! I'm living life half asleep."

"Yup. Half asleep, or maybe three-quarters. Or seven-eighths. But don't feel bad. Nearly everyone is operating that way, hanging by a thread."

"Geez. That's really depressing. But what's it got to do with rule 6? A or B?"

"Ah. I'm glad you asked. There is only one player."

"What?"

"That's Rule 6b. **_There is only one player._**"

"Only one?"

"Yup."

"You mean I'm alone?"

"Yup."

"That's not depressing — it's terrifying. I already felt alone, but now you're telling me I'm all there is?" Harvey fell silent. *That's just solypsism. Insanity. The voice really is nothing but me, my own confabulation.*

"Ah, yes and no. All I'm telling you is that the voice in your head isn't someone else."

"I thought you said you were God."

"I did, not that it did much good. But I am."

"Then you're saying that I don't exist?"

"Nope. We both exist. But there's only one of us."

"What on earth does that mean?" Harvey realized he was mentally shouting again, something he hadn't done since his last dialog with the voice. It was embarrassing, but he couldn't help it.

"You're me. I'm you. There's just one of us."

"You can't be saying I'm God. That's ridiculous."

"I am. You are. It's not."

Harvey sat back in the driver's seat. He was vaguely aware of gasping for air, and that his skin tingled as if all the tiny hairs were standing up. He didn't believe for a moment that he was God. But somewhere deep inside, he sensed some wild possibility he hadn't known before. He couldn't quite put his finger on it. This was too preposterous to digest.

"I guess I really don't understand anything about God," Harvey said.

"Get out of the car," said the voice.

"Right now?"

"Yes. Let's walk over to the beach."

Harvey stepped onto the tarmac, wondering if some miraculous vision was about to appear, and made his way through sparse traffic to the beach. He paused in the parking lot.

"Go on out into the sand," said the voice. "It's nicer out there."

He walked to the edge of the concrete, took off his shoes and socks, and trudged across the beach. He liked the hot sand between his toes. Half-way to the rolling surf the voice said, "Stop."

He stopped, wondering how many people would be able to share whatever he was about to see.

"Look up," said the voice.

Harvey looked up at the sky. It was the bright blue perpetual summer sky of Malibu, cloudless, with a bright fat sun just starting to approach the Western horizon.

"What do you see?" said the voice.

"Blue," said Harvey. "Blue sky."

"What else?"

"Nothing. It's all sky. High up, arching over everything. Out to the horizon."

"That's all?"

"Just sky," said Harvey, wondering if he was supposed to see something else.

"That's God," said the voice.

Harvey looked up again. The sky was as it always was in daytime, a luminous blue bowl, encompassing the whole world. *I guess that's what 'all-encompassing' really means,* he thought to himself.

The warm sun made him want to lie down and just stare up at the blue expanse. *That's God, eh? Could it be?*

He felt tiny, contained in familiar immensity. But he felt at home, too. *Is God really the sky? Isn't the sky just sunlight refracting in the atmosphere? How could the sky be God?*

"How can the sky be God?" he repeated, at the voice in his head.

"Well, to begin with, everything is God. But this is a good place to start."

The surf roared and hissed in a long gentle rhythm. *I'll have to think about this,* he thought. A long wave curled along the sand.

"Where is it?" said the voice.

Harvey jumped. "Where's what?"

"The sky."

"Well, it's up there, out there, all around."

"True enough," said the voice. "But where do you really see it?"

"Out there, like I said."

"But where are you experiencing it?"

"On my retinas?" What was the voice getting at?

"Not really. Are you inside your eyes?"

"No. I'm inside my head, I guess."

"And?"

"So I'm seeing the sky inside, in my mind's eye?"

"Why are you asking me?" said the voice. "Just look at where you are and tell me where the thing you're looking at really is."

"It's inside," said Harvey. "I'm seeing it in my mind, but it's an external image coming from my eyeballs, obviously."

"The sky is everywhere," said the voice. "And you see it inside."

Harvey waited.

The voice continued, "How can everywhere be inside?"

"I don't know!" Harvey cried. "I don't know what you're driving at. Yes, the sky is a sensory experience, so it's in my head. But the sky itself is outside, hundreds or thousands of miles away."

"You're so literal," said the voice.

"And you're just being poetic?"

"The whole thing is poetic, if you look at it the right way."

"That's no help. I still don't know what you mean."

"Somehow," said the voice, a little more slowly than usual, "you're able to spend your entire life looking through what you're calling your mind's eye, at your sensory movie screen, and seeing, well, everything. Even things so much bigger than yourself that you can barely comprehend them. Your entire vision of what is, of the universe itself, is inside."

Harvey waited again. It was often best just to wait.

"And I'm inside, too," the voice continued. "You and I and the entire creation. Inside your head. You and I are the same thing."

"But I know I'm not God!" Harvey exclaimed, for the second time.

"That doesn't make it true," said the voice.

In some non-verbal corner of Harvey's brain, or personality, an unexpected thought arose.

Maybe I am? he thought.

"Yo." said the voice. "Dig it."

Ω

Chapter 7

More

Important things continued blossoming all around Harvey's life, like the silent red flashes in a distant thunderhead. Their immediacy embedded him in an amalgam of tasks and events that defined pretty much everything. Being God was the last thing on his mind.

His work involved a lot of driving, as befits southern California life. Harvey's new BMW was his home now more than the house in Malibu. He was driving down the coast highway, and he thought, *Things have changed. I wonder if the rules still apply.*

"Damn right they do," said the voice.

Harvey nearly drove off the road.

"Man!" he said, "Don't suddenly yell in my ear like that."

"At least you're getting more comfortable with me these days."

"These days? It's been at least a year," said Harvey.

"Two years, in fact."

"That seems more like it." He drove deftly around a large truck, expertly avoiding a northbound soccer mom. "What were you saying?"

"I was responding to your musings about whether the rules still apply."

"I hadn't realized I thought that out loud."

"You didn't. We go over a lot of this stuff twice, don't we?"

"Yeah, I guess. Does that mean we're pals?" Harvey immediately regretted his remark, just in case it really was God.

"Sure we're pals, Harvey," said the voice, a little boistrously. "Sure we are. We've always been pals. We'll always be pals." The voice seemed to have taken on a very faint Bronx accent, and it made Harvey nervous.

"Did I go too far?" he thought, very quietly.

"Say what?" said the voice.

"My crack about 'pals'?"

"Of course not. Harvey, you've got to get it through your head that I'm not overly sensitive about things. I'm not just a gigantic version of yourself."

Harvey shuddered.

"Mainly," the voice continued, "I'm delighted that you're willing to interact. Most people just freeze and clam up. It makes imparting wisdom frustrating and inconvenient."

"Except you're immune to frustration, right?"

"I *am* frustration," the voice continued. Harvey made a mental grimace. "And love, and fear, and honor, and satisfaction, and bravery, and restlessness —"

Harvey cut him off. "OK," he said.

"I have to be careful what I say, though. Like just now when I said 'restlessness' you immediately cut me off."

"I'm sorry. I didn't mean to do that."

"I know. It just slipped out. It's OK. I'm still not offended."

"Good," said Harvey, with genuine relief.

"In point of fact," said the voice, "You couldn't offend me if you tried. And believe me, some very weird people have tried amazingly hard."

"I don't think I need to know about that," said Harvey.

"True." The voice paused for a while. "So, do you want to know the full answer?"

"What was the question?"

"Your question: Do the rules still apply."

"Ah, yes. It wasn't really a question, though."

"You weren't asking me, true, but it was still a question. And the short answer is yes."

"I guess that settles it, then."

"Except there's more."

"Don't rules either apply or not? What more could there be?"

"To start with, you've stumbled onto Rule 7: ***There are more rules.***"

"Uh oh. How many? Lots, I suspect."

"More than the stars in the sky," said the voice.

"That sounds pretty hopeless for mere mortals like me," said Harvey.

"Don't get down on yourself," said the voice. "For you, there are just *more* rules, not billions more. So it's really quite manageable."

"Are you going to tell me all of them?" said Harvey. "At the rate we've been going, I'll be dead and buried before we get through more than a dozen or so."

"I'll tell you the rules you need to know, but you have to kind of *live into them*."

"What does that mean?"

"You live a little, I give you a rule, you live a little more, I give you another," said the voice. "Like that."

"I see." Harvey thought about the earlier rules. Some of them had proven to be valid observations about the way things seem to work. Rule 3 had come in handy several times, in fact.

"Yes, Rule 3 is probably the most important one. Other than Rule 1, of course."

Harvey nodded.

"But there's more to it," said the voice. "Rule 7 has a footnote, so to speak. A disclaimer of sorts. A little fine print."

"Fine print?" Harvey thought the voice was uncharacteristically glib today.

"I have a right to be glib," said the voice. "And the fine print is just this: *Some rules subject to change.*"

"What? That's not fair at all. It's bad enough that a person may not even get the rules, and it's worse that there's always more rules …"

"There're," said the voice.

"Theirrr?"

"Nevermind. Go on."

"Well it just seems mighty unfair that even if somebody gets some of the rules, they may get changed. That makes it worse, knowing a rule that *has* changed, but not knowing it's obsolete."

"Who said anything about not knowing?"

"Well, if the rules are constantly changing, how would anyone ever find out?"

"Uh, what are we doing right now?"

"So you pop up and inform people whenever a rule changes?"

"I love the way you take every concept and stretch it into something ridiculous."

"Having rules that are constantly changing is what's ridiculous. It means they're not even rules."

"Who said anything about *constantly*?"

"Well, I …"

"All Rule 7 says is that there *are* more rules. It doesn't even specify that they apply to you, does it? And being subject to change doesn't mean *has to change*, does it?"

"I suppose not."

"Whenever you don't like what you're hearing, you extrapolate the original idea to some extreme so you can feel superior."

"Well, I …"

"And then you project the illogical extreme consequences onto somebody else, so you can feel magnanimous."

"Alright! So I'm a jerk. Obviously I can't live up to all your expectations; I can't even live up to my own."

"Actually, you're perfect living proof of all my expectations, and I love it." The laughter bells sounded softly in Harvey's head. "I'm just holding up a mirror. It's like when a toddler falls back onto his bottom, that expression of surprise and fascination. It's priceless."

"I guess I'm a toddler to you, aren't I"

"You bet you are! And what a magnificent one. All grown up and busy as a beaver."

"That doesn't make me feel very good."

"It will when you think about it later on," said the voice. "Nearly everybody likes to know I care about them."

"I still think changing the rules is unfair."

"Not if you haven't been told any rules."

"Geez," said Harvey. "That's harsh."

"It's true, though. Most people don't even know there *are* rules, so if a few rules change it makes no difference at all.

It's just people lucky enough to find out about the rules who might care, and, as you now know, I'm going to let them know what's changed. I'm a nice guy, all in all."

"Sometimes it's hard to believe that, the way things happen in the world."

"No doubt about it. That's why it's good to know some of the rules. You're a lucky man."

"But rules that change says something about the whole system, doesn't it?" said Harvey. "Doesn't it mean that you can't be certain of anything? That there's nothing consistent?"

"Very good point. Those could almost qualify as rules themselves, if they weren't mostly untrue."

"How are they not true?"

"You can indeed be certain of some things. You just have to understand what certainty is."

"Well if the rules are changing, how can you be certain about anything?"

"Only certain rules change, and most things remain consistent for your whole life. Sometimes it's you that changes, not the rule. But look at it this way. If I never told you a rule, how could I alert you that some rule or another has changed? You wouldn't know what I'm talking about."

"True. But what is there that isn't changing?"

"Me," said the voice. "For starters. And you, too, since you're a projection of me. We remain."

"I can't agree with that at all. I've been changing all my life."

"Have you? You've learned, and grown, and aged, but the inside you is the same one who sat in a pine tree twenty years ago. Isn't it?"

Harvey looked inside, trying to see who lived there. There was nothing to see.

"You can't see yourself without a mirror," said the voice.

"Sure, but then where's the mirror?" said Harvey.

"Me," said the voice. "Use me."

Harvey let his mind flounder around for a while, trying to imagine how he could use a disembodied voice in his head as a mirror for his inner self, and then gave up.

"Nice try," said the voice. "But by 'me' I don't mean this voice in your head. That's just a thought."

"So what do I look at?"

"You're not going to like the answer..."

"Try me."

"Just do not look," said the voice.

"I don't know what that means. And how would I do it if I did know what that means?"

"Well, it's not something you learn, either. But trust me, it will get clearer, and by and by you'll realize what I meant."

"Well, I'm afraid what you said wasn't much help."

"Like a lot of things, the benefit isn't always immediate."

"I'll have to take your word for it."

"Yes, take a crack at that. But now it should be pretty clear that all the rules are in your head. These aren't rules imposed outside by society, or by a jealous deity (whatever that is), or by a team of supernatural enforcers. These are simply the way it tends to work."

Harvey mulled. Mind-gnats swirled.

"And as you can see after even this small number of rules, it's complicated."

"Complicated. Yes, definitely. And vague, too."

"Perhaps you think rules have some kind of power," said the voice.

Harvey nodded immediately, without thinking.

"When your English teacher told you to use the Series Comma, that doesn't mean you can't omit the comma. What it actually means is that things go better if you use the comma. There's no punishment for missing commas."

"Outside of grammar school."

"Right."

"So just know that if you're alert, you can catch any new rules that come along. And rules that change."

"Right," Harvey said again.

"And if you're clear-minded, I can keep you up to date more easily."

"Right."

"Speaking of being alert, there's a red light up at the next intersection. And you're almost home."

Harvey had been driving for miles on autopilot. It was unnerving, but his street was just ahead and he was looking forward to seeing his wife and eating a bowl of soup.

Ω

Chapter 8

Thumbs

For the next several weeks, when Harvey returned to the car the voice was silent. He had to drive several times a day, but there was still no voice, and it was something of a relief. He was getting tired of scrutinizing everything. Eventually he concluded, with some relief and only a touch of disappointment, that the voice wasn't coming back.

A few days later, he was reading a book in the bathroom when the voice returned. "Hey," it said.

Harvey was a little upset. "What's going on? Why don't you come to the car anymore?"

"Oh," said the voice. "Did you think it had something to do with the car?"

"Well, that's the only place I ever see you now."

"Ah. You made a prediction. I'm not that predictable."

Harvey groaned. "It's not your unpredictability that's frustrating."

"Frustration is always based on the failure of predictions, isn't it?"

Harvey said nothing. Then he said, "Look, will you wait a minute for me to get out of here?"

"Sure. Why?"

"Well this is very embarrassing, to be talking to you in here."

"In here?"

"Oh come on," Harvey yelled, in his head. "In the goddam bathroom." He paused. "Oops. Sorry."

"Oh," said the voice. "I hadn't noticed. I don't pay attention to those kinds of details. But if you're uncomfortable, I'll wait." The voice was silent for a few seconds. "Don't rush."

Harvey fumbled around and finally made it to the living room of his Malibu house. He flung himself on the couch, trying to forget where he had just been.

"Why did you come while I was in there?" he asked, his irritation lingering.

"I don't come to places, Harvey. You should be able to infer things like that."

Harvey sulked, although he knew that every non-verbal nuance of his sulk was patently obvious to whoever was currently visiting inside his brain.

"I come to your awareness on the basis of time, not space. Circumstance, not location. Need, not expectation."

"OK, I get it," said Harvey.

"Well," said the voice, "you sound pretty receptive now for Rule 8."

"If you say so," said Harvey. "What's Rule 8?"

"***There are no rules of thumb.***"

"That's Rule 8?"

"Yup."

"But isn't that just a generalization?"

"No," said the voice. "It's not. It's just a rule of thumb. A good thing to remember. Something that usually proves to be true. Kind of an observation. It's almost not a rule." The voice paused again. "Of course," it continued, "all rules are a kind of generalization."

"Well, then, why include a rule of thumb in the rules?"

"Because for you it's a rule."

"But you just said it's also a rule of thumb itself?"

"Yes," said the voice. "For me it's whatever I want it to be. For you, it's a rule. For someone just thinking about it in the abstract, it's a rule of thumb that denies rules of thumb, a complete contradiction. This is the kind of stuff we both have to live with."

Harvey's head filled up with gnats, and for a while he was speechless.

Finally he said, "So you won't be coming back to the car?"

"Did I say that?"

"Well, you always come to me when I'm in the car now, and you never came any other time, until today. So naturally I assumed you preferred the car."

"That's a rule of thumb," said the voice. "First the tree, then the car."

"Yeah. Right," said Harvey.

"And there are no rules of thumb," said Harvey and the voice, in unison, which is a particularly unusual experience, hearing two voices at the same time in one's own head. They were both quiet for a while.

Harvey finally broke the silence. "Why is Rule 8 even worth mentioning?"

"I thought you'd never ask," said the voice. "The thing is, people like to come up with rules of thumb. They like it a lot. It's actually a hard-wired tendency."

"You built it into us?" said Harvey, astonished at the implications.

"If you want to put it that way."

"But then you have to tell us to ignore all the rules of thumb we come up with? That's kind of perverse, isn't it?"

"You could see it that way," said the voice, "but I don't. Besides, I didn't say to ignore rules of thumb. I only said there aren't any."

"But..."

"I hate to interrupt," said the voice, "but this is an important distinction: you can create something (a rule of thumb) that doesn't exist."

"What?" *Is he crazy?* Harvey's head spun.

"Of course I'm crazy," said the voice. "Why else would I create all this?"

Harvey paled. Even though he wasn't at all convinced that the voice was God, the notion that God might just be some omnipotent lunatic was deeply unsettling.

"Oh come on," said the voice. "Now you're going overboard."

"Well, you can't blame me," said Harvey, lost in circular reasoning. *If God made me so I go overboard, then how can he tell me not to go overboard. And if God made me so I have thoughts like this, including thoughts that I'm talking to God, then God is making the thoughts, too, and nothing makes any sense at all.*

"You're right," said the voice. "You're not making any sense. But let's back up. First of all, I'm not crazy — but I do have a sense of humor, and I was just kidding when I said that. And my point, before you went into a tailspin, was that you can create something that doesn't exist. I can't, but you can. That's what's really amazing."

"That *is* amazing," said Harvey. *And it still doesn't make sense.*

"Let's accept that Rule 8 is true, shall we? There are no rules of thumb."

After a while Harvey realized the voice was waiting for a response. "OK," he said.

"So now let's assume that one day you decide that if you go to a certain pine tree, I will speak to you inside your head."

"OK," said Harvey.

"Good. Now you've created a rule of thumb. Pine tree + Harvey = voice in head. OK?"

"Yes, but is it really a rule of thumb?"

"What else is a rule of thumb? This is a perfect example. And like all rules of thumb, it's something you made up, based on your observations."

"OK. I'll go along with that. But we're talking about rules of thumb as if they exist now, even though we started by accepting that they don't." Harvey felt a little swelling of pride at his dialectic skills. This time the voice wasn't that far ahead of him.

"Right," said the voice, very softly, and then continued. "What you've just pointed out is that this rule of thumb is in your head, but — according to me — it isn't real. Because there aren't actually any rules of thumb."

"So you're saying that I can create things in my head that aren't real."

"Precisely. It's hard to believe you didn't already know that."

"Well, I did, actually," said Harvey. "But you said the 'tree + voice' thing was a rule of thumb, after you had just said there are no rules of thumb. That's what sounds crazy."

"Good. Taking things that exist only in your head and assuming they're real — that's definitely one kind of crazy."

"OK."

"And you see how you can create things that aren't real. While I absolutely can't do that. Everything I create is real. As real as it gets, anyway."

"Can't you create thoughts in my head?" said Harvey. "Isn't that what you're doing right now?" *Ha! Now I've caught him.*

"Am I creating *your* thoughts," said the voice, "or just the thoughts that you call 'the voice'?"

Harvey paused. *Maybe I didn't catch him.*

"It was a good observation," said the voice, gently. "So now do you see the value of Rule 8?"

"I guess if you say it's true, but it sounds like a bunch of logic that isn't relevant to anything."

"The relevance is considerable: you don't make the rules."

"Well, I certainly don't make the laws of nature, if that's what you mean."

"That's part of it. But also, when you think you've discovered a rule, it might be hard to tell if it's a real rule, one of mine, or just a rule of thumb that you confabulated yourself."

"But aren't we always learning? Don't we gradually acquire more and more knowledge of the rules, based on experience?"

"Yes, and yes. But the thing to remember is that the real rules aren't ideas in your head. They're how things work, whether or not you're even aware of them. And they're there even if your knowledge and experience and learning are … shall we say … incomplete."

"So I should doubt everything that I think?" Harvey shuddered. *That's a sure-fire way to go really crazy.*

"Did I say to dwell on it? These rules aren't things you're supposed to obsess about. *That's* a sure-fire way to go really crazy."

"Didn't I just say that?"

"No, you thought it."

"That's what I meant."

"Then yes, you said it first."

"OK then."

"Good."

Ω

Chapter 9

Scores

Harvey's next decade was filled with the exercise of skills he acquired running the same department in the same company, year after year. The rhythm of office life, of evenings and weekends with his wife, of monthly meetings and annual holidays, was hypnotic. Routine became addiction, but career was complicated, with family, friends, associates, skills and expertise, even a little wisdom.

The seasonless life of southern California ebbed and flowed, punctuated by the usual fires, quakes, and mudslides. Getting ahead gradually became irrelevant: he was far enough ahead.

Harvey was sitting in his back yard in Malibu watching a small flock of parrots fluttering around a spindly palm tree. *How long does this go on?* he wondered, and then thought, *Until I get somewhere, I suppose. I wonder if I've been doing it right. I could get more aggressive. I could probably double my income if I play my cards right.*

The distant drone of leaf blowers drifted through the neighborhood. *But for what?* he thought. *Haven't I made it by now?* He looked at the back of his house. *This is all pretty good, actually.*

A sinking feeling swept over him. Maybe this wasn't It at all. He kept missing huge chunks of his life.

"I'm blowing it, aren't I?" he said, out loud. The parrots froze and eyed him uneasily.

"I wouldn't say that," said the voice.

"What?" said Harvey, looking around. Then he saw there was nobody there, and relaxed. "Oh, it's you."

"'Tis I," said the voice.

"Wow," said Harvey. "I'm afraid this time I really had completely forgotten you exist."

"Do I?"

"Good question," said Harvey. "How would I know?"

"Well, you're talking to me. That's a hint, I should think."

"Not really. We've never really established that I'm not just randomly schizophrenic."

"You mean MPD?"

"Sure. Sorry."

"But you're trying to decide whether you've made it or not."

"Yeah, pretty much. Things have been going along pretty well. But I can't tell if I'm getting closer to the goal."

"What's the goal?"

"That's the thing: I don't really know. I'm just doing what I think I should be doing, but there's no master plan, and there doesn't seem to be any way of knowing if it's OK or it's all a big mistake."

"Scores aren't announced during the game," said the voice.

"Well, I'm doing better than a lot of people these days."

"That was Rule 9."

"What was?"

"Rule 9: ***Scores are not announced during the game.***"

"Another rule? This one doesn't seem terribly useful." Harvey thought back, trying to remember some of the other rules. "Not many of the rules seem to be very useful, come to think of it."

"You remember them all?"

"No, only a few. Sorry. They just don't stick in my mind for very long."

"Not important," said the voice. "Things you learn have an effect, whether or not you remember each thing individually."

"So what good is Rule 9? It sounds like you're saying there *isn't* any way to tell if I'm actually doing well."

"I wasn't saying that, but it's a valid interpretation of the rule."

Helpful as always, thought Harvey. And then he thought, out loud, "But all this is pretty good, yes?" He mentally waved his arm at the back yard and his large stucco house, with its 'peek' at Santa Monica Bay. "It must mean I'm doing something right."

"It certainly does."

"Compared to some people, anyway."

"I suppose," said the voice.

"That sounds like you have reservations."

"Not really..." The voice had a distinctly tentative tone.

"Are you messing with me again?" said Harvey. *Why is he always doing that?*

"What's the value of knowing your score?" said the voice, in a more serious tone.

"Isn't it good to know how I'm doing?"

"Of course it is, but how do you know?"

"From the score, obviously."

"You'd like to find out how you're doing in life by comparing yourself to other people?"

"Not just *comparing*," said Harvey. "Although it *would* be interesting to know where I stand."

"So you just want to be judged, is that it? By someone else? Aren't you the best judge of how you're doing?"

"I can never tell how I'm doing," exclaimed Harvey. "That's the problem."

"Then you're in favor of there being a score."

"I guess so. If God is doing the scoring."

"Who else would be?"

"Just about everyone who knows I exist!"

"Right," said the voice.

"Still, wouldn't it *have* to be important for me to know how you're judging me?"

"It would be if I were judging you."

"You're not?"

"I don't judge," said the voice. "It's a myth."

"Really?" Harvey was astounded. He had never heard of such a thing. Even though he didn't believe in God anyway.

"Why would I judge? I'd be judging myself."

Harvey had to think for a while. He stared at his house, not seeing it. Then he said, "Then what's the point of a score in the first place?"

"It's not something that has a point. It's automatic. When you do something, the effect is there, willy-nilly."

Harvey sat quietly. "I haven't heard that since my grandmother was alive," he said.

"Your grandmother talked to you about the score?"

"No. Willy-nilly. What a weird expression."

"Your grandmother was a great person," said the voice. "She was very proud of you."

"Why, if you don't tell us the score, do you bother keeping track?"

"I don't keep track. It keeps track of itself. And Rule 9 is perfectly clear — Scores aren't announced during the game."

"Why not?"

"Because they'd be completely misleading. They have no value. They're just a side-effect of doing things. Of learning, or missing the point."

"So I won't know the score until after I die?" said Harvey, rubbing his head.

"That's one way of putting it," said the voice, and then after a pause, "If you still think you need to know. But you also don't know what anyone else's score is. Or if points are being added or taken off."

"Points get taken off, after you earn them?"

"Sure, of course. You've known about brownie points since you were a kid, haven't you? You win some, you lose some."

"This whole score setup sounds like a complete waste of time," said Harvey, still rubbing his head.

"It is," said the voice.

"They why are you telling me all this?" said Harvey, out loud, waving his actual arms.

"You brought it up," said the voice.

Ω

Chapter 10

Prizes

The next week at the office was slow. The same issues and uncertainties simmered and the same activities moved along. The same personnel caused problems and solved problems. By the weekend, Harvey was ready for a few hours in his Adirondack chair, where he could gaze between the adjacent homes at his expensive 'peek' at the ocean. His wife had gone out, as usual, for her Saturday hour at the driving range. Harvey didn't like golf.

It was a quiet morning, without the usual on-shore breeze. The distant surf was barely audible over the sporadic rush of traffic on the Coast Highway.

As soon as Harvey set down his coffee mug, the voice spoke.

"You seem dissatisfied with our last conversation," said the voice.

"Well, I was trying to figure out if I'm doing the right thing with my life, or maybe going in the completely wrong direction." Harvey paused. "And then you turned it into a brain-twister about scores."

"Harvey, we've been calling it the Game of Life since the beginning, haven't we?"

"Sure, but it's a metaphor."

"Is it?"

"Isn't it?"

"You tell me," said the voice.

"Well, if it's a game, it's a pretty damn serious one."

"That's up to you. A game's a game."

"You said yourself we all have to play."

"Sure, but are you playing or working?"

"Working. In fact, it's a lot of hard work."

"But what are you working at?" said the voice.

"What do you mean?"

"Are you working at playing the game?"

"Yes! That's exactly what I'm doing. What everybody's doing."

"Working at playing?"

"Yes."

"Forgive my saying so," said the voice, "but that really doesn't make sense. How can you work at playing?"

"Well, you do what you have to do, and it isn't necessarily fun, is it?"

"Rule 3," said the voice.

"I know, I know," said Harvey. "You always throw that one back at me."

"Well, I'm not always throwing it at you because I like throwing things," said the voice. "I'm throwing it at you because it answers half the questions you throw at me."

"Then how is it a game if you have to work to play it?"

"You think baseball players don't work?"

"Of course they do."

"And they don't enjoy baseball?"

"Well, yes, obviously. But that's different. Baseball is a game."

"What makes it a game more than the Game of Life?"

"For one thing, it's pointless. You just do it for fun."

"First, it's not pointless, or you and millions of other people wouldn't pay so much attention to it and pay the players like movie stars. And second, you *could* play the Game of Life for fun, too."

"But life is so full of horrible things, suffering, accidents, cruelty, disasters. It doesn't sound like fun to me."

"What about your house? No fun in that?"

"Sure, yes, but not everybody gets a house, especially a big one in a great location."

"Isn't your house a consequence of your own planning, creativity, and achievements?"

"Yes, but that wasn't playing around. I had to work hard to make it happen."

"You strove to play the game well, and you got your reward."

"So my house is a prize?"

"Yup."

"And my fancy car?"

"Yup. Your loving wife, too. Even this cup of coffee you're drinking."

"You're saying that everything positive that happens is a prize?"

"More or less."

Harvey pondered. "Then is everything bad that happens a punishment?"

"We've been over that," said the voice. "I don't punish."

"Then what *are* the other things that happen? They're certainly not prizes!"

"Harvey," said the voice in a slightly patronizing tone, "Not everything is a prize or a punishment. That's ridiculously simplistic and you know it."

"Then what?" Harvey was getting exasperated again.

"Things happen," said the voice. "The whole system is running quite nicely. Sometimes you're going along with it, and sometimes you're trying to go in a completely different direction. That leads to different levels of enjoyment. I should think that's plain enough."

"What about hurricanes? Are they because everybody on the Atlantic seabord is going in the wrong direction?"

"There's no need to try and cross wits," said the voice. "It's not a matter of winning an argument, you know."

"Sorry," said Harvey. "But still, hurricanes?"

"Weather," said the voice.

"Just weather? Really?"

"Really."

"All that suffering is just an accident?"

"There's nothing accidental about weather," said the voice. "It's a complicated system, though, so it's hard to know what's going to happen next." The voice paused, and then said softly, "But then, it's always hard to know what's going to happen next."

"But the people!" said Harvey. "They lose their homes. Their possessions. People drown. And it's all just a coincidence?"

"Who said it's a coincidence?"

"If it's 'just weather' then it sounds mighty coincidental to me. Or at least pointless."

"You're getting righteous, Harvey," said the voice.

"Well, all these people's lives are being ruined!"

"You know that? You've looked at each one of the people in a hurricane and seen how their lives were ruined?"

"No, of course not..."

"Then you're generalizing, aren't you?"

"Yes, but..."

"Each person is different, Harvey," said the voice. "You know that perfectly well."

"Yes," said Harvey. He was starting to feel like he was back in grade school.

"And each situation is different, too."

"Yes."

"And each outcome is different."

"OK."

"And things keep happening to each person *after* the storm."

Harvey nodded, in his mind, but it seemed to work.

"So it's complicated," said the voice.

"Yes," said Harvey, tentatively. This wasn't clarifying things the way he wanted.

"More complicated than the weather," said the voice.

"Right."

"Much, much more complicated. So you can't judge the lives of a million people on the basis of one weather report, or one casualty statistic on the news."

"I guess not."

"Sometimes misfortune leads to greater good fortune," said the voice.

"I suppose so."

"So you might even get a prize, as you put it, just for being in the right place at the right time."

"Being in a hurricane is being in the right place?"

"It might well be," said the voice. "Especially if you get a prize for it. Someone comes to your aid and lifts your heart higher than it's been in decades. An insurance company sends you money. A house that was a fire-trap gets demolished and you move into a safer one."

"OK," said Harvey. "Sometimes good comes from a catastrophe. But what about the people who drown."

"Like I said," said the voice. "Some people may get a prize."

"Drowning!?"

"There are prizes," said the voice, "and then there are Prizes."

Harvey looked down. *Metaphysics again,* he thought.

"The point," said the voice, "is Rule 10: ***Prizes may be awarded randomly.***"

Harvey was, once again, slightly stunned. It was hard making sense out of the whole Game at once. Maybe it really wasn't worth analyzing, if there were never any good answers.

"There are some very good answers," said the voice. "But an answer is only as good as the question."

Harvey thought some more. "That's completely unfair. What's the point of awarding a prize if it's random?"

"Well, the rule overstates it. They only *appear* random."

"You're saying it's too complicated to figure out, though, which is basically the same thing."

"For you, perhaps. Not for me."

"But it's so ridiculous! Some people bust their asses and get nowhere, and other people cheat and steal and end up with millions."

"End up?"

"Sure, they live like kings, but they don't deserve a penny of it."

"First, they don't live like kings: they live like rich people. Second, you don't know what they deserve. You're making people into caricatures. And third..." the voice paused.

"Third?" said Harvey.

"You don't know how they end up, do you?"

"You mean they'll get their just deserts in the end?"

"I'm not saying."

"You mean you won't say?"

"Nope."

"Nope you won't say, or nope that's not what you meant?"

The voice fell silent, and Harvey relaxed a little.

"Then how on earth..." Harvey began.

"If you want to understand the game better, you won't get anywhere by analyzing other people's prizes."

Harvey remained silent.

"You're better off looking into your own prizes. Other people's prizes won't ever make much sense."

"I guess not." *Especially if you're not going to explain.*

"Have you got a couple of thousand years?" said the voice.

"For what?" said Harvey.

"An explanation. This kind of knowledge doesn't fit well into English sentences, you know."

"German?"

"Very funny," said the voice, with the very distant clink of one bell. "But think about it more sensibly."

Harvey waited.

"It makes no sense to give *everyone* a blue ribbon, because then it's not really a prize. Besides, you've all been given all kinds of prizes, but if you notice that everyone got one, you'll decide it doesn't count."

"But can't you give some prizes explicitly?"

"Of course. But it rarely helps. How'd you like to be lugging the Stanley Cup while you're trying to skate?"

Harvey chuckled at the image of a huge padded hockey player skating furiously down the ice with a three-foot tall, thirty-five pound trophy under one arm.

"But still," Harvey said. "Prizes are inspirational, don't you think?"

"Indeed they are," said the voice. "That's why some of them are more obvious than others."

"But don't you think the randomness just confuses people?"

"If I built all this so it wouldn't confuse people then believe me, there'd be nobody here."

Harvey started to say something, but the voice was gone in an unusually prolonged flurry of bells.

Ω

Chapter 11

Events

It was a few weeks before Harvey finally got back to the Adirondack chair. This time it was facing the hillside behind his house so he could look for coyotes. A neighbor's cat had disappeared and there were still plenty of coyotes living in the Santa Monica mountains. Harvey had never seen one close up.

There was a rustling in the scrubby bushes just up the hill from his garden wall. He leaned forward, and thought he glimpsed something moving behind the foliage. Then there was a glint of light. *A dog-tag?* he wondered. *Maybe it's somebody's dog.*

Then the glint grew into a broad glow inside his head, and Harvey remembered his first experience with the voice, back in New York, sitting up in the pine tree.

"We left a few things unresolved," said the voice.

"Are you doing the inner light again?" asked Harvey.

"It's kind of neat, don't you think?" said the voice.

"Yeah, but why bother?"

"Oh, it's no bother!" said the voice.

"I mean, why do it."

"Just for fun. It gets your attention, in a nice way."

"That it does," said Harvey, settling back in his chair. "What was unresolved?"

"You weren't all that happy about random prizes," said the voice. "Or scores, either, as a matter of fact."

"No, I'm not. It seems like things should be more comprehensible."

"That's what I want to clarify," said the voice.

"You actually have some answers?"

"My answers are more like rules," said the voice. "From your point of view, anyway."

"I was afraid of that."

"There's one more thing about prizes."

"What's that?"

"Rule 11: ***Your prize might not be for your event.***"

"That's idiotic," exclaimed Harvey. Then he said, "You already said they're random, so why mention that they might also not be yours in the first place? It's chaos!"

"Let's start at the beginning," said the voice. "I never said that prizes are random. I said they may be awarded randomly."

"What's the difference?"

"It's all in your point of view. You can't analyze them, any more than you can analyze the weather, so they seem random. But they're not. And neither is the weather."

"Alright," said Harvey, marveling at how good the voice was at splitting hairs.

"And I never said they might not be yours. Any prize you get is most definitely yours. If it weren't, you wouldn't get it. That part's simple enough, isn't it?"

"Simple enough for a poor human, I guess," said Harvey.

"Good," said the voice, ignoring Harvey's tone. "So let's get back to the point. When you get a prize, like, say, a big promotion at work, it might not be because of that fantastic report you wrote last quarter."

"OK," said Harvey.

"So that's it. Your promotion might be due to the boss's wife liking your necktie at the Christmas party."

"That's a bit fanciful, don't you think?"

"Sure, but it's an analogy. Do I have to explain analogies?"

"No. I take it back."

"You can't, but I'll get to that later. Rule 11 just clarifies why you can't always make sense out of the things you call prizes."

"But these good things that happen aren't always just out of the blue," said Harvey. "Like this house. If it's a prize, then it certainly was for my event."

"True, if your event was 'getting a house.' But was it?"

"Sure. My wife and I were both working towards it for ages. It took planning and self-discipline and a lot of other things."

"During all that time, there was nothing else you were trying to achieve?"

"There were plenty of other things. We tried to have children, without any luck, *by the way,* and we had to deal with some illness, and there were a few little earthquakes, *as you know.* And a lot of things at our jobs."

"Then how do you know that getting the house-prize was just for your efforts in that project? Maybe it was a prize for being kind to each other all those years, through all those challenges."

"Well, it could have been, I guess."

"Look at it this way, if a prize is for just one thing, then where do you draw the line? How can you separate that one thing from all the other things going on in your life at the same time?"

"You can't, I guess."

"Precisely. And there's another thing."

"Which is?"

"Consequences take some time to come about."

"Consequences?"

"The results of your actions. The prize, if you like."

"Doesn't the system respond immediately? If you drop a ball, it falls instantly, doesn't it"

"It *starts* falling instantly, but it takes a while to hit the ground. And some actions have very long-term consequences. Just look at history."

Harvey mulled it over. "I guess I see what you mean."

"So eventually, some action, or more precisely some overlapping pattern of multiple actions, brings about a visible consequence. A prize is awarded. But you may naturally assume it's the result of whatever has happened most recently."

"I guess so."

"It's like a gambler who thinks he rolled a natural because he blew on the dice just right."

"Yeah."

"I guess it's pretty clear now that there isn't much point obsessing about prizes," said the voice.

Harvey nodded.

"Actions are like musical notes. Some of them last a long time; others are brief and clear. They add up, and they lie on top of each other, making chords. Your whole life is a huge chord, made up of all the actions you've ever made. Your chord spreads out and makes more harmonies with other people's chords."

"Ah," said Harvey, trying to imagine.

"It's quite beautiful."

"I guess it would be," said Harvey.

"Oh, it is," said the voice. "You'll see."

Ω

Chapter 12

Want

It was Thanksgiving, although even after decades in Southern California Harvey still had hadn't gotten used to the complete absence of fall, winter, and spring. The house had finally become silent after all the in-laws and guests left, and his wife had gone off to explore the pre-Christmas sales.

Harvey sank into the Adirondack chair with a huge sigh of relief. Holidays were good, but exhausting. He took a deep breath, and immediately reached down to loosen his belt. He had eaten far too much bread dressing and apple pie.

"Phew," he muttered. "Why do I always do that?"

A post-prandial stupor was spreading through his mind, and he welcomed the drowsiness. The last few weeks had been more tiring than usual.

He woke up a few hours later, feeling, as his long-departed father used to say, like a boiled owl. *That's the trouble with naps*, he thought. *They always leave me feeling hung over.*

A gentle salty breeze was drifting up from the beach, bringing just enough dampness to give the illusion of an autumn chill. But the sun was still shining, and Harvey settled comfortably into his chair for another nap. *Maybe it will clear my head,* he thought.

"I can clear your head, if you like," said the voice.

"Huh?" Harvey looked around and then realized it was 'the' voice and not 'a' voice. "You can clear my head, you say?"

"Yup. Shall I?"

"Well, sure, why not?"

Instantly a feeling of alertness and sharpened perception dawned in Harvey's mind. It felt like he'd had a good night's sleep and awakened without an alarm clock, and with something to look forward to.

"Nice!" he said. "How did you do that?"

"Like this," said the voice, and Harvey glimpsed something bright and clear, deep inside himself.

"What was that?" he asked.

"That's you," said the voice.

"But what did you do?"

"I didn't do anything. Well, I did in the sense that I just pointed at it."

"You pointed at me?"

"At the you inside. You know that inside you're never tired or dull, don't you?"

"Gadzooks, no! Half the time I'm just plain worn out."

"But who is worn out?" said the voice.

Here we go again, thought Harvey.

It's worth it, thought the voice.

Harvey jumped. "Did you just *think* something at me?"

"Yup. It's just like we normally do, only softer."

"But it was like me having the thought, instead of you saying something inside my head."

"It's still confusing for you, isn't it?"

"It sure is. And it's unsettling to think that someone else can be putting thoughts into my head that aren't my own."

"That's not what happened," said the voice. "I just spoke more softly. You heard that thought the same way you hear everything else I say. If you're listening, of course."

"Well it seemed pretty different to me," said Harvey diffidently.

"You didn't answer my question," said the voice.

"Which one?" said Harvey. "Oh, *who* is worn out?"

"Yes."

"Well I want to just say 'I am worn out,' but I'm sure you'll disagree."

"Right."

"So I guess it's whoever is thinking my thoughts that thinks I'm worn out." *This is getting dangerously loopy.*

"Right again. And how do you know what that thinker is thinking?"

"Say what?"

"How do you know you're having a thought, regardless of who's doing the thinking?"

"Well obviously I hear it," Harvey said, straightening up in the chair. *This is slightly ridiculous.* "I hear all the thoughts in my head. How else could I think?"

"Ah, but you're conflating thinking and hearing."

"I am?"

"Sure. When I just put that thought into your head, you heard it. When you put thoughts into your head all by yourself, you hear them. So the putting and the hearing aren't the same thing."

"Hmmm," said Harvey, and then suddenly felt stupid about making a thinking sound in his own head. "But then if I'm doing the thinking, who hears the thoughts?"

"You've got it backwards. Your body does the thinking, and *you* hear the thoughts."

"Oh, I don't think so," Harvey began, and then the recursion began to short circuit the logic center in his brain.

"When I say it's your body," said the voice, in a reassuring tone, "I don't mean your arms and legs. I mean the delicate machinery of your nervous system. The most advanced part of it, in fact."

"Advanced machinery?"

"Thinking isn't something just anyone can do," said the voice. "Pretty much only people. Around these parts, at any rate. You won't find rocks that think. Or even Bird of Paradise plants."

"Don't animals think?"

"Nope. They have thoughts, but they don't do any thinking."

"That's self-contradictory!"

"No. Thoughts arise in a squirrel's awareness while he's doing something. But he's not asking for those thoughts. They just arrive. Humans ask for it."

"I thought you said I wasn't the one doing the thinking."

"Your body is doing a lot of it, but you're instigating the process much more than necessary."

"Then isn't that just another way of me doing the thinking?"

"Are you driving if you have a chauffeur?"

"Oh alright. But if I'm not doing the thinking, what am I doing?"

"Not much," said the voice.

"Well, not now. I was dozing. But most of the time I'm pretty damn busy."

"Your body is, and your mind, lord knows, but not you. All I did a few minutes ago was point at you the listener, you who hears the thoughts, and your brain fog cleared right up. That's because you're not your brain, not your mind."

"Did you just say 'lord knows'?"

"It's an expression."

Harvey sat in silence for a few minutes. Thankfully, the voice had nothing to add to his mental gyrations. Gradually the circular reasoning stopped circling and a new question popped up.

"If I'm not doing the thinking, and it's all the body, then why does *it* do things?" And then he thought to himself, *Where did that thought just come from?*

"Desire powers the whole thing," said the voice. "And desire powers desire, too."

"Oh?"

"Sure. Everything you do comes from some deep desire."

"I thought 'the whole thing' meant everything. Literally."

"It does. But it's easier to understand if you look at yourself and what gets you moving."

"But there are lots of things I do because I have to, not because I want to."

"Desire is a very basic thing, Harvey. It doesn't really have much to do with wanting."

"I don't know what you mean. I want to get the car fixed, because I desire to have a working car. What's the difference?"

"There are a million ways to deconstruct you wanting a working car, and of course getting it fixed is dependent on that, but it's a different desire, isn't it?"

"Sort of. But it's based on the same thing."

"Right. This just shows how certain desires spawn others."

"OK."

"That means there's a hierarchy of desires. When you want a bowl of ice cream, it's probably not because you're hungry, right?"

"Well, in that case yes. I just want the pleasure. But pleasure can't be the basis of everything that happens! Ninety-nine point nine nine nine percent of the universe is inanimate stuff. You can't be saying that the rocks and atoms are all in search of pleasure!"

"Well, I *could* say that," the voice began, and then trailed off, leaving Harvey anxious that the whole discussion was about to go sideways.

"But I won't," the voice said cheerfully, "because I don't want to give you a headache."

"You mean it's true, but you're going to spare me?"

"I'm not going there," said the voice. "And that's that."

"Then where are you going?" said Harvey, a slight whine entering his mental voice, which he helplessly regretted.

"Let's keep it on the human level for now," said the voice.

"Yes, let's," said Harvey.

"Then consider Rule 12: ***The more you want.***"

"That's not even a sentence."

"Well, it used to be just 'the more you want,' but that seemed too terse. I like terse, but since Rule 12 is so central to everything that's going on in the world, I decided to give it a little more structure."

"So that's not Rule 12?"

"It's the short form. The full official form of Rule 12 is ***The more you [x], the more you want; the more you want, the more you [y].***"

"What the, uh, heck are you talking about?"

"Don't you think the official version is clearer than the short form?"

"No. Why don't you just tell me what it means?"

"It just means that whatever you're doing, it will lead to wanting more. And at the same time, the more you want things, the more stuff you'll be doing."

"I would have to think about that for a while."

"Fine. But for now, it's pretty easy to grasp, isn't it?"

"Can you put it another way?"

"I've already put it three ways. How about you tell me what you don't get."

"It's just not that easy to understand. In fact I think I don't understand it at all."

"The more you eat, the more you want to eat. The more you want to eat, the more you eat. How's that?"

"But the more I eat, the more full I get. So I *don't* actually want to eat more and more."

"Then why, if you don't mind my asking, are you a bit round in the middle?"

Harvey blushed, and wondered if he was blushing inside. "Well, I do eat more than I should. And I should get more exercise."

"That's what they all say," said the voice. "But when you get full, don't you still want more?"

"No — I'm full. I can't eat any more!"

"But you would if you could?"

"Oh. Yes, I guess so."

"So the desire is still there. You still want more. You just can't find room for it."

"I suppose you're right." *As usual.*

"Have you noticed who does the wanting?"

"Who, me?"

"Yes. And who does the other part?"

"What other part?"

"The 'I don't have room for another bite' part."

"Oh. The body I guess. My stomach."

"Good. So 'you' want more, but your body doesn't."

"Not right then it doesn't."

"Later on it does?"

"Sure. Every few hours it starts reminding me to eat."

"Then it's the body that wants more?"

"Yes. It's the body that gets hungry."

"I thought you said it was you wanting more, but there wasn't room."

"Well, I did. I guess sometimes it's me, and sometimes it's the body."

"Rule 12 doesn't specify who does the wanting, or the doing. But I think you do understand it now, right?"

"Yeah, I suppose."

"Good."

"But you said desire powers everything. Rule 12 is just about people. You said so yourself."

"Indeed I did," said the voice, with what sounded like a hint of pride. Now and then Harvey got the distinct impression that the voice really was proud of — he had to think a moment — well, *it.* As if maybe the voice actually was God. Or at least had convinced itself that it was. *But God wouldn't succumb to base human emotions like pride, would he?*

"Who said pride is a base emotion?"

"You heard that?" said Harvey. Then, "Of course you did." He scratched his head. *What was I thinking?*

"You were thinking that there's got to be more to it than just desire, powering the whole universe. Is that about right?"

Harvey was relieved to avoid another theological wrangle. If his instincts were right, then the voice wasn't God because God wasn't real. But if he was wrong, then a misguided theological discussion could be dangerous.

"Hey, Harvey, give me a break, please," said the voice. "I don't zap people for speculating about things they can't understand. But we were talking about desire."

"Right," said Harvey. *Can I trust an unidentified voice in my head?*

"Yes, you can. Now listen. The desire that drives you to eat ice cream comes from a more basic desire to experience pleasure. That comes from the desire to be happy. That comes from the desire to experience *living*. That desire is fundamental to life itself. Every living thing seeks survival, and seeks to express its nature."

"Plants *want* to grow?"

"Not like you do, obviously," said the voice. "But it's built into their biology, and it's expressed in a plant-like fashion. You don't want to call that desire, but I dare you to find the line separating fundamental biological imperatives from plain old desire."

"But what about the rocks, the lifeless asteroids?"

"Lifeless?"

"Surely nothing is alive on a fifty-foot chunk of rock frozen in outer space!"

"Nothing you'd recognize, anyway."

"Can we not go there, either?" asked Harvey.

"No need," said the voice. "It's more basic: the photons and electrons express the stuff they're made out of. Whatever you want to call that stuff, it's the basis of the way atoms and such actually behave."

"Behave?"

"Function. Operate. Do their thing." The voice clearly didn't want Harvey getting any pickier than he already was. "If something in that realm behaves exactly like a photon, then it is a photon. There's nothing else to identify it other than the way it works."

"OK," said Harvey, cautiously.

"And it's just the way that the atomic stuff behaves that results in the more complex stuff, and eventually biology. And eventually you, wanting ice cream."

"You make it sound so simple," said Harvey.

"Don't," said the voice, very quietly, almost beyond the threshhold of Harvey's perception, "patronize me."

Harvey gasped and then held his breath.

"Just kidding," said the voice. "You're too easy."

Harvey exhaled.

"And I've overloaded your brainpan this time. Sometimes it's hard to stop. You ask a good question, and then I can't resist answering it. But each answer calls for an explanation, and it accumulates a little too much for comfort."

"Well, I..." Harvey began, while some polite platitude began to take shape in his pre-frontal lobes.

"It's Thanksgiving," said the voice. "Relax. Think about this stuff some other time. Take a nap."

The game's going to be on soon, Harvey thought.

Ω

Chapter 13

Specifics

A great deal of time can pass when important things are happening. Harvey's life had been full of such things, and it had taken a long time. He had married, not had kids, been promoted several times, bought a house, then a better one, and moved up in the world. The decades were passing, and when Harvey looked back, it reminded him of a time-lapse movie of the Grand Canyon, long shadows sweeping across the colored landscape, night skies appearing and disappearing, suns and moons and stars wheeling overhead again and again, permeated by a deep mysterious silence.

Then his wife died, and the grief he once thought he had missed made up for lost time.

For the first time in four years he wondered where the voice was. He listened for it inside his head, but there was just silence.

Weeks after her passing, when he finally could go for a few hours at a time without weeping uncontrollably, the voice said, "Hey."

Harvey was sitting in the living room, staring at the TV, which was off. Nine out of ten thoughts were about his wife, now gone for nearly a month, but he still couldn't fully believe what had happened. He didn't want another enigmatic dialog with the voice — he was too tired to think — but it was a kind of relief to have a thought that wasn't about her, and didn't immediately send his body into anguish.

"Now's not a good time," he said, half hoping the voice wouldn't hear him.

"I understand," said the voice. Then it fell silent.

After a while, Harvey said, "You still there?"

"Yup."

After another while, Harvey said, "What are you doing?"

"Just being," said the voice.

"Oh."

"I didn't think you were in the mood for talking."

"I'm not."

"Good," said the voice.

Ten minutes went by. Then Harvey noticed that the whole time he had been wondering when the voice would speak again. And at the same time, he realized that the pain had abated.

"Feel better?" said the voice.

"Yes, but only because I wasn't thinking about her," he said.

"You don't need to think about her all the time."

"I can't help it."

"Part of the time you can't," said the voice. "When the brain is reorganizing everything there will be a lot of thoughts about her. But when you have a choice, there's no need to dwell on it."

Right. My wife just died and I don't need to dwell on it. Sure thing. Harvey let his attention wander back to the blank TV screen. *We used to watch programs together.*

Finally Harvey blurted, "Why the hell did you do that to her?" Usually he wouldn't have been so blunt, but now he didn't care.

"I didn't do anything," said the voice. "She, along with everything else, was just going along with the rules."

"That's ridiculous," exclaimed Harvey. "She didn't want to die! I didn't want her to. Why would *you* want her to? She never did any harm to anyone!"

"Nobody wants to die," said the voice. "Including me. But dying isn't a punishment. Everybody dies."

"I know," said Harvey, wearily. "Nobody said life is fair. Rule 100, right?"

"That's not a rule," said the voice. "It's a platitude." Pause. "And besides, you have no idea what's fair unless you know the whole game, not just your piece of it. Fairness applies to everybody, so unless you understand everybody else's situation, you can't tell if anything is fair, can you?"

"Then what's the difference between a rule and a platitude? It seems like a lot of the things you've been telling me are platitudes."

"No. They're rules. Platitudes are truisms. They're useless. They're just statements that sound good. Whether or not they sound good doesn't have anything to do with being true."

"I still don't see the difference."

"'Everything happens for a reason' is a platitude. Maybe you meant 'aphorism.' Aphorisms are usually just definitions, but it's not entirely crazy to think of the rules as aphorisms."

"Sheesh," said Harvey.

"Confucius said, 'The hardest thing of all is to find a black cat in a dark room. Especially if there is no cat.' That's an aphorism."

"Oh," said Harvey, trying to unravel the Confucius quote. "Did Confucius really say that?"

"In Chinese he did," said the voice. "And a lot is lost in the translation. But not all aphorisms are rules, so you're better off if you just stick to mine, and call them rules."

"Fine," said Harvey. The blank TV was getting more and more interesting.

"What makes these Rules special is that they are absolute. They're not clarifications of specific details or instances. They apply to life itself."

Harvey suddenly realized he was arguing with a voice in his head about platitudes, while his whole life had just been turned upside down and he could barely function. "Why on earth are we talking about platitudes at a time like this?"

"That's the second time you've mentioned the time," said the voice.

"So what?"

"Time is the whole problem," said the voice.

This is getting ridiculous. I really, really don't want to be sucked into another dialog.

"Then don't say anything," said the voice. "Let me do the talking."

"Is there some way I can stop you?"

"No."

"I figured as much."

The voice fell silent for a few minutes and Harvey's agitation settled down. Then the voice said, "When you think about what has happened, you feel grief."

No shit.

"And when you think about the implications for your life, your future without her, you feel grief."

Ditto.

"And when you listen to my voice, you don't feel grief. You feel anger, or resentment, or restlessness, but the grief goes away."

"Great. The voice of God can distract me from my grief. That's a bleak observation if ever there was one."

"It's not what I say that's distracting you from grief," said the voice. "It's not even a matter of distraction."

"Then what is it?"

"I'm inside," said the voice.

"Inside what? What on earth do you mean?"

"My words are inside your head and they're happening right now."

"Of course your words are inside my head. We've been doing this for half a century."

"The words are in your mind right now."

"So what? Of course they are."

"They're not memories."

"Obviously."

"The words aren't what you think I *might* say, are they? They're what I'm *actually* saying."

"You have always had an amazing knack for stating the obvious," Harvey said, and then felt guilty, and then wished he didn't feel guilty, and then his depression won over and he gave up analyzing his feelings.

Before Harvey could sink back into them, the voice said, "People have a knack for not noticing the obvious. That's what 'obvious' means. Transparent. Self-evident. Not worth further consideration."

"I know what 'obvious' means."

"What's not obvious is that you feel horrible only when your attention is on the past or the future."

"I'd say I feel horrible all the time these days."

"Most of the time. Not all of it."

"OK, ninety-nine percent of the time. That should be enough."

"But you don't feel horrible when your attention is on something in the present."

"I feel pretty horrible right now, thanks."

"But you're not weeping, your throat isn't taught and aching, your nose isn't running, your stomach isn't in a knot..."

"So what?"

"That's how your body responds to grief thoughts. Your thoughts right now are of bitterness and depression, but not of grief."

"Bitterness and depression are just another kind of grief."

"They're completely different emotions, and you know it. And if you look more closely at my words, even the bitterness goes away."

"No it doesn't. It just makes me more irritated."

"You're not being entirely honest, Harvey," said the voice.

Harvey replayed the last sentence, 'You're not being entirely honest, Harvey.' *Well, then, how do I really feel, right now? Am I grieving, or bitter, or depressed, or what?*

For a long moment, Harvey didn't think at all, waiting for an answer.

Then he thought, *Good grief. There's no grief. I feel completely normal.*

Slowly, Harvey framed his next thought. *All I'm doing is looking inside to see how I feel.*

He thought about his wife's passing, and all the months of suffering and fear. Instantly, his whole body convulsed in anguish, and he grabbed a pillow and sobbed uncontrollably.

Then a flicker of curiosity struck him, and he glanced again inside, not at the feelings, which were all in his gut, his throat, his eyes, his heart, but at what was just inside himself, at nothing.

The grief stopped. And it stopped like flicking off a light-switch.

This is more than a little amazing, he thought. *I wonder if...*

Harvey thought about his situation, living without his wife, never seeing her again. Another wave of sheer physical torment swept over him. He looked back inside again, and again the grief had gone silent.

He remembered the last few years of sickness, his wife's passing, and the grief slammed into his heart like a grenade. Then he looked inside at himself, to see if he could survive this pain, and the grief ceased.

He thought about what life would be without her, and the grief swept through him, cramping his throat and knotting his gut. He was alarmed at the intensity and glanced again at his core, looking for damage. No grief. Just silence.

"Don't wear yourself out," said the voice.

"But this is incredible," said Harvey. "I'm sobbing and wailing and then I just glance at myself, and the grief stops cold. What's going on? How can it just cut off like that?"

"There's no grief in the present," said the voice.

"Is that really true? It seems so simplistic."

"You've just seen it's true. You look at the past: grief. You look at the future: grief. You look at how you feel right now: peace."

"But how does that work? How can my whole body just shift gears instantly like that? It usually takes half an hour for the pain and crying to wear off."

"The pain and crying aren't wearing off. Your body is just getting tired of doing all that work."

"It is exhausting, that's for sure."

"There's a lot of mental reorganizing to do when someone important goes out of your life. The first meal without them, the first shopping trip, the first cup of coffee. It's all got to get sorted out in your brain. All your priorities have to get readjusted."

"No kidding."

"When that's happening, your attention goes onto the past, or the future, and you feel grief. When you have a choice, you can look at the present instead."

"So I should resist thinking about the past and the future? That doesn't sound like a good idea."

"I'm not telling you what to do. I'm describing how it works."

"So I can dwell on it if I like?"

"Sure. You can wail and carry on for years. You can make it a way of life. Lots of people do."

"But what if I don't want to? It's a big gyp, not even being able to think about her without getting tortured."

"The choice is yours, every time you have another thought. To entertain it, or let it go and move onto the next one. But if you *fight* it, that's just a negative motivation — you're still entertaining it."

"This is Rule 3 again, isn't it?"

"Correct. To enjoy is optional."

"So is there a rule for today?" said Harvey, half hoping there wasn't.

"Just a simple one. Rule 9 is ***Player-specific rules may apply.***"

"Wow. That's not at all what I was expecting. Not after all this life-coaching business."

"We've just been talking about the obvious, remember? Obvious, but not always noticed. That's not the stuff of rules at all; it's just paying attention to your own experience. Rules are abstract."

"Is Rule 9 coming up now because of what just happened?"

"Yup."

"My wife had different rules?"

"Yup. She sure did. Some rules the same, some different."

"Did she die because she broke a rule?"

"You can't break these rules; they're like the laws of physics. And I already said, death is not punishment. I don't punish."

"What do you do, then, teach? Correct? Enforce karma?"

"No, no. Good heavens, that would be utterly tiresome."

"Then what?"

"I make the rules."

"I guess that should be obvious. But what else? What about people? Behavior? The game itself?"

"It's all just rules. Everything is made out of rules. Rules inside rules inside rules. But we'll get to that later."

"I think I don't understand."

"Definitely not!" Soft bells. "But you will, so don't worry about it."

"Why did she die?"

"You already know. She was following the rules. Not your rules, though. That's why it's so hard to understand what happens, especially to other people."

"I want to be able to think of her and be happy."

"That will come."

"I guess so."

"I know so. Look inside."

Harvey glanced in again. Silence, as before. Was it always silent inside? Behind the thoughts? *How do you keep out the noise? The clouds of thought-gnats? The pain and fear and confusion? The uncertainty? What am I supposed to do?*

"Nothing," said the voice.

Ω

Chapter 14

Mulligan

Gradually he stopped shopping for two, comparing life before and life after her death, talking aloud to her, imagining how she would react to his current life. Priorities changed; value systems simplified; his career moved toward full monopoly of his attention.

There was an imperceptible change in the cycles of corporate weather and a different climate emerged.

Negotiations were underway to sell Harvey's shares in the company. Apparently he had decided to retire. He wasn't aware of having made any such decision, but now there seemed to be no other sensible thing to do. *I wonder if I'm doing the right thing,* he thought. Then, hoping he could bounce his decision off someone, he pulled his seventh BMW onto the shoulder by Zuma Beach, and shut off the engine. *I'd like to talk this over with you,* he thought, imagining the voice might come when he called.

Not surprisingly, there was no voice. But he realized, perhaps for the first time, that the voice was almost the same when it wasn't speaking to him as when it was. Maybe that's what it had meant by Rule 6B. What was the voice, when it wasn't speaking? Was it listening? Was it there, or did it go away when it wasn't talking to him? Was it anything, or did it exist only when it spoke? The voice always seemed to come out of the silence at the back of his head. Maybe the silence itself was the voice. Maybe the silence was Harvey.

"Will I go crazy if I retire?" Harvey said aloud, to the dashboard of his car. The Bluetooth GPS replied, "Contact or destination not found."

Harvey realized he had missed another whole year. *How many now?* The thought was abrupt and unexpected, and a pang of fear rose up with it. *I haven't been paying attention,* he thought. *Decades! I get so busy. And now she's been gone for a year, too. I must have missed something. A lot of things.*

He stared across the highway at the beach and the ocean and the sky. *I really screwed up,* he thought.

"No you didn't," said the voice.

"You're here?" said Harvey. "You haven't left for good? I keep forgetting..."

"You know I'm always here," said the voice.

"Theoretically, I guess, but you're not always there when I need you."

"Yes I am."

"No, you're not. Where were you when my wife passed away?"

"I believe we had a conversation just after, didn't we?"

Harvey winced; he hated when the voice asked rhetorical questions. It didn't seem fair. "It's over a year and I've still only barely begun to feel normal," he said.

"I know that. I have my eye on you. I want you to be happy."

"It doesn't feel like you do."

"I know. Feelings are often misleading."

"I just wish it had turned out differently."

"I understand."

Harvey sat still and kept quiet. Inside he felt a weird mixture of sadness and regret.

"Why did you do that to her?"

"There's some misunderstanding, Harvey. I don't do."

"Well, somebody did. Somehow she got sick, and it's your creation. It's your responsibility, what happened to her. Or anything that goes wrong, for that matter."

"Interesting idea," said the voice. "And would you also blame me for all the good things that happen?"

"Sure, of course. Everything that happens."

"And everything that happens, that includes gravity?"

"Yes, of course."

"So you're blaming me for creating a system that includes both positives and negatives."

"That's right," said Harvey, wondering if he was falling into something sticky. He didn't really want to let God's culpability slip away.

"Why do you choose to blame me when something goes wrong, but you don't thank me when something goes right?"

"Well, I guess because when something goes wrong, it really stands out."

"Exactly. If you're going to blame me for anything, you really have to blame me for everything."

"OK. Then I do. But still, it begs the question. Why would you let something like that happen to such a person? She was so kind and generous; everyone loved her. I loved her."

"And that's the point you just made," said the voice. "I didn't let something happen to her. I created the universe, including everything that happens in it."

"Then why create a universe that does that?"

"Now, *there's* a good question," said the voice.

"And now you're going to give me one of your dramatic last-word exits and not answer that?"

"Oh, I'll answer it, but you won't like the answer."

"OK, try me."

"It didn't really happen."

"That's ridiculous. She's dead, and I'm miserable. And it definitely happened!"

"Ah. It happened to you. But did it happen to her?"

"What do you mean? She's the one who died. Of course it happened to her."

"Something did. But you're the one who's complaining."

"How can you blame me for complaining when my wife dies? And how could she complain if she's not here?"

"Actually, I'm not blaming anyone for anything. You're blaming me for everything."

Harvey sank back in his seat.

The voice went on. "But you shouldn't try to speak for someone else. You don't know where she is now, or what was really happening inside her. You only know the outside."

"So all you're really saying is that I should think about Rule 3 again, and find some way to enjoy the fact that she died?"

"No, no, no, not at all," said the voice in a peal of bells that lasted longer than usual. "That's ridiculous. You're being ridiculous to prove your own point."

"Well then, where does Rule 3 apply?"

"It applies because, if you know Rule 3 exists, then when you do have a choice to enjoy something, you can make that choice."

Harvey was silent.

"Rule 3 means that you are not obligated to suffer. Anytime you want to, anytime it's possible, you may choose to enjoy."

"I guess I see what you mean," said Harvey. "Last time you told me this I was pretty distracted." He glanced inside. There was nothing.

"What did you just see?" said the voice.

"Nothing," said Harvey.

"Grief? Sorrow? Resentment?"

"Not at that moment," said Harvey.

"Is it possible for you to enjoy the absence of grief?"

"Well, yes, of course it is. It's a huge relief," said Harvey.

"Good," said the voice. "Then look inside, and see no grief, and enjoy."

After a few minutes, Harvey said, "There were so many things I should have done, should have said. Not done, not said..."

"Those things don't matter," said the voice. "She wasn't thinking about them anyway."

"I just wish I could take back some of that stuff. I never meant to hurt her."

"Everybody bumps into someone else's ego now and then. It's inevitable."

"Yeah, but I know I said things I shouldn't have. Things I didn't even need to say. Just stupid remarks. Stupid stuff. I wish I could take it back."

"Obviously you can't take it back. It's in the past, whatever it is. The ripples are moving on outward no matter what."

"There's no way to fix anything after the fact? Even for you?"

"I don't do anything that needs fixing. In fact I don't do, so the concept is meaningless."

"But if I say something hurtful, and immediately regret it, can't I try to take it back?"

"Sure, you can try. But you can't take anything back. Once an action takes place, it's out there."

"That's depressing. Some people have done some really horrible things."

"True. But there's more to it than what you can see."

"Like what?"

"The scale of what's going on in creation is so far beyond anyone's ability to comprehend that there's no way to begin to explain it."

"God can't even explain his own creation?"

"Explain it to whom?"

"To me. Part of your creation." *That should be obvious, shouldn't it?*

"It is obvious, but you just answered your own question."

"I did?"

"How can I explain this nearly infinite field of diversity through nearly infinite time to one individual mind?"

"I guess you can't. I'm little more than an insect in the grand scheme."

"There's where you're mistaken," said the voice, with a few bells in the distance.

"You just said I couldn't comprehend it."

"I did, and you can't. But that's not because you're stupid. It's because you *are* it."

"Huh?"

"Every part of creation is the whole creation."

"What?"

"Every moment of time is the whole history of the universe."

"You're getting way beyond me, I'm afraid."

"The point is," said the voice, "that you can understand the creation only by understanding that you're not separate from it."

"But I can look at it. Doesn't that make me separate?"

"It makes you think you're separate. But the point is that the whole thing is bigger than thoughts. Bigger than concepts. Bigger than ideas."

"Then how could anybody ever understand it? Even super-beings with a billion years of evolution behind them?"

"They can't. Nobody can."

"So I was right."

"The complexity of the overall system is far, far beyond any being's ability to grasp."

"Yeah."

"The scale of the thing as a whole, or the sweep of time, these are incomprehensible."

"I get it," said Harvey.

"But the nature of what *you* are is inseparable from what *I* am. I've told you before: we are one and the same. So as you get to know me better, you get closer to grokking the whole enchilada."

"Grokking? Really?"

"Hey, it's a good word. Do you know a better one?"

"No. And enchilada? Are you joking again?"

"Again, it's a word that conveys the idea. Don't be a snob."

Harvey relaxed a little, marveling that God would bother to use slang and colloquialisms in the middle of explaining the universe. Then he wondered why God would even bother explaining at all, since he already knew nobody could follow the explanation.

"You're following it, aren't you?"

"Your words, yes, but I still don't know what you're talking about."

"The point you should grok is simply that when you do something you want to un-do, there's so much more to it than you could possibly understand that there's no point trying to analyze it. Blame me for creating the whole enchilada, if you like, but it's not going to be understood whatever you do."

"So what should I do if I realize I just committed a horrible act?"

"Well, before you commit a horrible act, I'd recommend that you remember Rule 14."

"Which is?" *Do I always have to ask?*

"Rule 14 is **You can't take it back.**"

"Ah. I see. In the heat of the moment, I'll try to remember that."

"No need to be cynical."

"No, but really, how likely is it somebody would ever remember a thing like that when he's fighting mad, or drunk, or whatever?"

"The universe gets along fine with probabilities, so, as usual, I wouldn't advise you to worry about it. Just hope you remember — that's enough."

"OK," said Harvey, although he wasn't entirely satisfied.

"Realistically," said the voice, "you'll never be entirely satisfied. Not until much later, anyway."

"What happens later?"

The voice ignored his question. "There's a second part to Rule 10," it said.

"Another two-part rule, eh?"

"Yup. Part two is, **Do-overs may be allowed.**"

"Do-overs? What's a do-over?"

"You know. A mulligan. A retry. You take another stab at it, whatever it was that went sideways."

"But you said you can't take it back."

"You can't. The act is done. The ripples are spreading away through the whole universe. You can chase after them, send out some correcting influence, or you can let them go. But you can't take it back."

The voice paused while Harvey tried to assimilate.

"Do-overs are another thing entirely," said the voice.

"So if I lose my temper and punch somebody in the nose, obviously I can't un-punch him, but I can still take a do-over? That really doesn't make sense."

"Right you are! It makes no sense at all."

"But you just said..."

"You aren't very good at catching the little words, are you?"

"What?"

"The second part of the rule is that do-overs *may* be allowed. If you try something and fail, you can try again. But if you punch someone in the nose, there's not much point in taking a mulligan. You'll just end up punching the guy a second time, which will probably be much worse."

"I see. Why not just make the rule say, 'Do-overs are allowed wherever possible'?"

"That's subtly different. It implies do-overs are always allowed if they're possible."

"But doesn't..."

"You're getting lost in the language. It's a common pastime, but pointless. Just stick with the rule. I didn't word them this way by accident."

Harvey sat quietly in the driver's seat, idly fingering the maple steering wheel. Traffic whizzed by.

"So what about all the things I regret saying to my wife? She's gone, so a do-over won't accomplish anything. I'm just stuck feeling guilty, aren't I?"

"Well, you know this much," said the voice. "First, what's said is said. Opportunities missed are over. You can't take anything back. And since she's gone, any do-overs will have to be for yourself. Or for someone else. Or for everyone else."

"I just have to keep trying, is that it?"

"Not exactly trying, in the sense of forcing yourself to do something that doesn't come naturally. But in the sense of 'now you know.' Now you see things differently; your priorities have changed."

"But I should try a little, shouldn't I?"

"Not try. Care."

"Care about next time?"

"Right on," said the voice.

A tractor-trailer roared by and Harvey's BMW rocked in the truck's tailwind. The voice was gone.

Ω

Chapter 15

Trees

A few more years slipped by, and Harvey did end up selling his stake in the company. He moved to a year-round cottage at Lake Tahoe, and continued trying to adapt to life by himself, without her, and without even an office-full of people depending on him.

Living at the lake was more peaceful and healing than Harvey had anticipated. As usual, his anticipations had proven utterly unreliable. The thin clean air was effortless to breathe, and the huge blue lake, surrounded by its own private Sierras, was a constant inspiration. But an inspiration for what? He hadn't done anything since retiring here. Worse yet, the company he left had fallen on bad times, and didn't look like it would survive the recession.

Before leaving California, he had half-heartedly started planning a new company, something he could do his own way, the right way, something that would bounce him out of bed every morning like summer itself used to do when he was a kid. But the motivation just didn't run deep enough. He couldn't seem to get it off the ground.

Here at the lake, doing big things, doing it right, no longer seemed necessary. Sometimes it felt like he wasn't even doing the physical activity of his own life. Was his personality running on autopilot now? Was he getting too detached?

It didn't take long, living at the lake, to discover Sand Harbor, and a tiny cove where he could clamber onto a large rock that was completely surrounded by water. The rock was always warm in the sun, even in winter, and he could sit there and gaze at the lake for hours.

He loved the way the afternoon sun glinted off the waves. It reminded him of the first day in the pine tree in New York. He could easily envision the way the glinting light had swept into his head, filling his mind with light.

"It's a big circle, isn't it?" The voice was quieter than usual, and seemed almost like a natural part of his thoughts.

Sort of, he thought. "Did I just think your voice, or is that actually you?"

"It's me."

"Hi," said Harvey.

Surprisingly, the voice said nothing. *That's a twist,* he thought.

"Don't spoil it," said the voice.

He watched the lake rippling in the breeze. He wondered if the voice was watching, too, through his eyes.

"Yes," it whispered.

His thoughts turned back to his old company in LA. *What should I have done? I tried to set the company on a better track, but there was just so much entrenched resistance. Nobody likes change, I guess. My god, they fought every improvement I tried to make.*

"You may plant a tree," said the voice.

"I tried to keep it going," Harvey replied.

The voice was silent.

"I was thinking of starting a new company, but now I don't think it's worth the energy."

"If your work doesn't give you energy, then consider a different line of work."

"I'm not sure what gives me energy nowadays. I'm 60, and there's a lot less energy than there used to be."

"There's still plenty of energy to do what needs to be done, though," said the voice.

"I'm not sure what that would be."

"You don't need to be sure. Go in the direction that you're leaning."

"You know," said Harvey, looking up at the mountains that surrounded Lake Tahoe, "During the heyday of Virginia City they cut down all the trees."

"Yes, I know."

"The Washeshu must have thought the white men were insane."

"Indeed they did! People do the damnedest things."

"But they all grew back, didn't they?"

"Some of them. Not many new ponderosas and jeffreys yet."

"No. Lots of sugar pine, but most of them are dead."

"Bark beetles."

"I wonder what we could do to fix this," said Harvey.

"It will fix itself," said the voice.

"But how? Half the new growth is dead."

"Fire," said the voice.

"But that would be terrible!" said Harvey.

"Getting caught in it would be hard," said the voice. "But that's how the old forest got here. Ponderosas don't mind a fire now and then; they're built for it. Clears out all the dead sugar pine, fertilizes the soil, frees up space. It will be beautiful."

"But people will lose their homes. All these towns and villages could be destroyed. That would be a huge tragedy."

"Maybe it won't happen that way," said the voice.

"I sure hope not."

"Rule 15 is about trees," said the voice.

Harvey snapped out of his doomsday vision. "Trees?"

"It seems like a good metaphor," said the voice.

"What's the rule, then?"

"Rule 15: ***You may plant a tree; you can't grow a tree.***"

"Wait a sec..." Harvey considered the terse statement. "You're saying I can plant a tree, but I can't make it grow?"

"Yes, but I didn't say 'make it grow' did I?"

"You said I can't grow a tree. What's the difference?"

"You can start something, but you can't control the outcome. You can try to steer your company back to profitability, but you can't make it happen. You can plant a tree, but the tree has to do the growing."

"So this is the rule I should have known three years ago."

"Right."

"What good is the rule if you don't tell me until after it applies!"

"Sometimes that's the only time it will make sense to you."

"But then it's too late!"

"Not if it applies again at another time."

"Oh."

Harvey looked again at the forested mountains framing the lake. The setting sun was casting a deep red-orange glow along the western ridge. He hoped the forest wouldn't catch fire, even if it was good for the jeffrey pines.

"I see what you mean about the tree," said Harvey.

"Yes," said the voice. "They take care of themselves. But there are other factors."

"Like us," said Harvey, in a gloomy tone.

"They needed the wood."

"But they destroyed the forest!"

"You want more?"

"More what?"

"Forest?"

"Well, yes. Look at it. It's not a forest, it's a tinder pile."

"You want more ponderosas?"

"Yes!" Harvey paused. "But I don't want a forest fire!"

"You absolutely have my permission to plant a ponderosa. You absolutely lack the ability to make it grow."

"But..."

"You can nurture it, but that's external to the growing. You can water it and protect it from frost, or whatever else you think might help, but in all cases you're only making changes to enable the tree to do its own thing more successfully. You're not doing its thing yourself. You're not even directly helping."

"The tree's own biology does the growing, not me. So if it lives or dies, it's not my fault."

"No, not at all. Living or dieing could certainly be your fault, just like this forest. But when it comes to the growing, you can't grow it. You can help, or ruin the outcome by messing with the situation, but you can't do tree growing."

"I understand. The tree does all the growing."

"Actually, it doesn't. I do."

"I knew you were going to say that."

"Yes, but of course I don't really do anything. It's all pre-set."

"Are we going to talk about free will again?"

"No. Did you want to?"

"God, no!" Pause. "Sorry."

"You don't have to keep apologizing for using the word 'god.' It's always good to think of me. I'm not easily offended; in fact, it's impossible. At any given moment, throughout the universe, you can't imagine how many beings are berating me for this and that. Being omnipotent, though, it truly cannot bother me. And being omniscient, I can't help loving them all anyway."

Harvey didn't know what to say.

Ω

Chapter 16

Singing

The rock at Sand Harbor had become a surrogate for Harvey's pine tree in upstate New York. When he sat on that rock, just barely surrounded by the lake, he felt like he did on the fat branch ten feet up the big white pine. The trees at the lake were huge by comparison, and he never seriously considered climbing one. He would have needed a ladder to get to the first branch.

Another decade flowed through his life, but this decade was filled with small events, moments of clarity, and many hours just going for walks, or watching the lake and the mountains. Harvey kept in touch with old friends, and sometimes they came to visit. He wondered how often they were really just visiting the lake.

Harvey wasn't doing much hiking in the Sierras now, but he did make a short pilgrimage to the rock at least once a week, weather permitting. The voice had come to him there, now almost ten years ago, and he was always half hoping it might find him there again. But after so many years, these strange occasional conversations with himself, or with whomever, were beginning to seem like fantasies.

His life was definitely winding down. He didn't enjoy thinking about it, but he knew that life in the mountains wasn't going to be practical for much longer. There was a pretty decent elder-care center in Reno that some friends recommended. But moving there would have to be a last resort.

He chuckled to himself at the play on words: his last resort.

"Still here?" said the voice.

"Ah! You're back," said Harvey, unexpectedly glad to have company. Even disembodied company of questionable reality.

"Waiting for the proverbial fat lady to sing, eh?" said the voice.

"I suppose that's it," said Harvey, suddenly realizing that he had been standing without moving for several minutes. He sat down on the rock to catch his breath.

"The interesting thing is," said the voice, "that the fat lady will not sing."

"That's a definite?" said Harvey.

"Yup. She won't sing because it turns out she doesn't sing."

"What does that mean?"

"She doesn't sing because she can't! She's not a singer. No chops. Can't carry a tune."

"Oh. Is that it." Harvey looked at the ground. "I had hoped if she wasn't going to sing that there might be a better reason. A more interesting reason, that is."

"There is one additional reason. I don't know if it's any better though."

"What's that?"

"She's left the building," said the voice.

"Oh lord," said Harvey, fully cognizant of the ambiguities in his remark.

"The fat lady has left the building," the voice reiterated.

"I got it," said Harvey.

"Perhaps not," said the voice. "You've been waiting for something that was never going to happen."

"Too bad that's not a rule."

"It's Rule 16. ***The fat lady will not sing: the fat lady does not sing (the fat lady cannot sing). Besides, the fat lady has left the building.*** It's the wordiest rule in the book."

The voice seemed unaccountably proud, which happened now and then. Harvey wondered if it was just his own interpretation of the tone of voice. It was hard to tell, especially since the voice and the tone were both just parts of Harvey's own internal world.

"No, I am a little proud of that one," said the voice. "It's not elegant, but it's in the language of the times."

"It is that," Harvey admitted. "Is it really your intention to invoke Elvis?"

"In your set of rules, yes. Why not?"

"I never much liked Elvis."

"I know. Gets your attention, doesn't it? That means it will stick in your mind."

"There's not a lot of the game left, for me to forget this one."

"You'd be surprised."

"I would?"

"You will. But I won't spoil it for you."

Harvey listened to the water lapping at the edges of his rock. He knew the voice wasn't going to give away any of the great secrets of life. It apparently wasn't his style.

"Oh, I've given you plenty of hints over the years," the voice said.

"Well, they haven't shed much light on what's next," said Harvey.

"It'll be easy," said the voice. "And fun."

"Whatever you say."

"Just don't waste your time. Especially this late in the game. There's no point just waiting for anything, is there?"

"Godot?"

"Ha!" A faint ripple of bells. "Nothing to be done, eh?"

"My god, you *have* read that? I finally got around to it last year."

"No need to read. Samuel and I are one."

"He wouldn't have liked your saying that, I don't think," said Harvey.

"He wouldn't have admitted liking it. But he knew Malloy and Mallone were the unnameable. So he wasn't very far off."

"But Lucky's speech. If you're not found, man just wastes away."

"Only some men do, and Samuel wasn't one of them. His art was about compassion, not about his beliefs."

"I wish I had done some art."

"There you go, into the past again. Don't let it tempt you at your age. There's so much past to get lost in, but the future is so rich in comparison."

"It seems more brief than rich."

"Well, that piece of the future is brief. But after the fat lady sings, it's a whole new ball game."

"I thought you said she never sings."

"You're right. I was violating my own metaphor. The thing is, there's no point waiting for the Big Payoff."

"You mean there's no point at all? No big secret to life? No revelation at the end?"

"It doesn't work like that. But there is a big secret, and I'll tell you."

"Say it!"

"The big secret is that the payoff isn't part of the game. It never is. It comes after you stop playing."

"So you're also saying there's something after this life."

"Obviously."

"It's not obvious to me."

"It's obvious when the time comes."

"Yes, and that's obvious, but not very helpful."

"There is so much more to it than what you see here."

"Why is it hidden from us, then?"

"It's not hidden. You just haven't opened your eyes wide enough."

"How do I do that?"

"By doing just exactly what you have been doing."

"Living my life?"

"Right."

"And then life after life?"

"More like life after dream."

Ω

Chapter 17

Winning

The real mountains were off in the distance now, and the lake was somewhere to the South, high above the city. But it wasn't so bad in Reno. The elder-care facility was clean and efficient, and the staff feigned an adequate friendliness. Some of the oldsters were interesting, when they had enough energy to interact. But they kept disappearing, one by one.

I am slip-sliding away, thought Harvey.

He was sitting in a big lounge that the center insisted on calling a solarium. It reminded him of the alien habitat bubble in *Slaughterhouse Five*. The desert sun streamed through huge windows all around, making his eyes ache. He hauled himself out of the armchair and stepped shakily to another chair in a patch of shade.

Last year, at 79, it was obvious that living by himself was no longer viable, so he moved from the lake. It wasn't a happy decision, but without a family there were no other options.

Has life really been reduced to this? he thought. *Nothing but a daily routine, with no goals or challenges?*

The shady section of the solarium was slowly moving East. *I'll have to move again in about fifteen minutes,* he thought.

I guess that's the challenge now. Maybe I can talk them into putting up some shades.

He had spoken to some of the staff about window shades during his first few months here, but they insisted that shades would contradict the purpose of a solarium.

"Enjoying your patch of shade?" said the voice.

Harvey sat up and looked around. A handful of elderly men and women sat quietly around the room, apparently spaced as far apart as possible. This was the first time the voice had come to him in public.

"They're not paying any attention," said the voice.

"I guess they're not," said Harvey. "But I'll have to be careful not to actually vocalize."

"I'm sure if you did, nobody would notice."

"Probably not. Muttering is standard fare around here." Harvey checked his thinking process to make sure he wasn't speaking outside his head. *I wonder if I was speaking out loud in all those other dialogs,* he thought.

"Not to worry," said the voice. "You've always been quiet as a mouse."

"Thanks."

"Thinking without vocalizing is good practice."

"How so?"

"It gets you closer to thinking without verbalizing."

"All thinking is verbalizing!" Pause. "Isn't it?"

"Not at all. Staring at the lake and feeling the sun isn't verbal. You don't have to be thinking, 'I'm sitting at the lake' inside your head." The voice paused. "Do you?"

"I miss the lake."

"I know. It's as beautiful as ever."

"Thanks," said Harvey, with a touch of bitterness.

"I meant that you can still think about it in all its glory," said the voice. "No fires. Just mountains and streams and trees and some tourists now and then."

"Now that I'm in this, uh, *place*, are we just going to chit-chat? That's all anyone seems to do here."

"Not at all. I came with an important rule for you."

"Really. I didn't think there's a whole lot of time left for rules. Don't much need rules from here on out, do I?"

"There's all the time in the world. There always is. Don't rush things."

"Oh, believe me, I'm not rushing." Harvey glanced at the dozens of armchairs. *Nobody rushes in here.*

"That's what people are always trying to do, though," said the voice. "It's what they think they have to do."

"Well, don't they?"

"Absolutely not. Work hard, even if the goal is impossible, perhaps — but don't rush."

"What's rushing got to do with it?"

"You rush, you screw up."

Harvey smiled. "Then why isn't this a rule: 'Don't rush.'?"

"It is," said the voice. "But it's on a different list. Lots of other lists, in fact."

"Why not mine?"

"You learned not to rush by yourself, so you don't need a rule. Can you imagine the size of your list if it had all the things you need to know? My god!"

"Wait a sec..."

"What?"

"You said..." Harvey paused. The voice was silent. "Never-mind."

He still likes to mess with me, Harvey thought, knowing full well the voice heard every ripple in his head. Then he realized he had a real question, one he hadn't ever considered asking before.

"What's the verdict, then?" he asked. "Who won?"

"Won what?" said the voice.

Harvey almost yelled, and then thought, very forcefully, "The Game!" *Duh.*

"Just checking," said the voice. "As for winning or losing, you can relax. You won."

"I won? Doesn't that mean it's over? But I'm still here."

"Alright, you didn't win yet, but you will."

"Wow. You're giving it away before the fat lady doesn't sing?"

"I'm not giving anything away. This is Rule 17."

"Rule 17 is that I won? That's not even a rule."

"Rule 17 is **You can't lose.**"

"Oh." Harvey's head started filling with thought-gnats again. *Wow. It's been years,* he thought, among all the other thoughts. But the gnats dispersed quickly.

"Are you relieved?" said the voice.

"Not relieved. More like disappointed. It kind of makes the game meaningless."

"Meaningless? You don't feel your life had any meaning?"

"If I know I'm going to win, then why bother to play?"

"The joy of the game..."

"Yeah, I know. It's in the playing. But if there's no actual winning, then why call it a game? It doesn't make sense."

"True. From where you sit, it can be pretty incomprehensible. But at least you know you can't lose, and for a lot of people that would be a big load off."

"Telling me I can't lose just makes the whole thing a big waste of effort."

"But you didn't know you can't lose. So you tried to succeed."

"That's my point. It's like you cheated."

"How did I cheat?"

"By not telling me the game is pointless. By letting me get so ... involved."

"The game isn't pointless. And I did tell you. It's Rule 17."

"Yeah, now you tell me. What good is that?"

"You'd rather not know? You'd prefer to go on thinking that you still have to win, wondering what will happen if you don't?"

"What would happen if I didn't win?"

"The same thing. That's the point of Rule 17. If you can't lose, then obviously you can't really win either."

"But why make us play? Besides, I got so much wrong, I couldn't possibly have won if it were a real game."

"First of all, it's not a real game. Second, you're in no position to judge. I am, but I don't. So you played because you believed you had to, and, in fact, you did have to."

"I had to?"

"Rule 1."

"Oh yeah."

"If I had told you Rule 17 back in New York, you would have still had to play, but you also would have thought your life was pointless. That takes all the fun out of it."

Harvey thought for a while. Or did he? Nothing came out in words, inside or out. *Is that thinking?*

"You still have such a charming way of putting your mind into a spin," said the voice.

"Sorry."

"No, no. I love it. It's part of what makes you you."

"So I won," said Harvey. "But I don't know the score."

"Good. Rule 9. But remember what Rule 9 was all about."

"I can't remember the whole conversation."

"Just that scores also don't mean anything until *after* the game. And by that time you're in a better position to make use of them."

"It may take me awhile to get used to not winning."

"Not losing."

"Same thing. Neither one. Now the game is incomprehensible again."

"No more than it was all along. Nobody said you had to win anything. You're hanging an awful lot of existential angst on the word 'game.'"

"Then what is life anyway?"

"You'd rather it be a game?"

"That's not what I meant."

"I know. You've just asked the Big Question, and answers to those questions aren't found in thoughts. The equipment responsible for making thoughts just can't make thoughts that size."

"So where's the answer, if it's un-thinkable?"

"I'll show it to you. But not right now."

"Gee, thanks."

"Because right now I want to get you ready for it. 'What life is' is not winning or losing. It's also not the game, not the process."

"Well, I guess we've established that it isn't the game. But I still think you could give me a hint."

"The answer requires stepping out of the process. The real game is what's not the process. And, that's why you can't lose."

"I definitely did not get what you just said."

"But doesn't that make it more fun again?"

"More fun? Not knowing?"

"More fun than thinking it's meaningless."

"Yeah, I suppose so." Harvey scrunched back into his chair. The solarium was still ablaze with sunlight and his sheltering shadow had almost completely moved away. "But where's the fun in..."

He looked around inside his head. The voice was conspicuously absent.

Ω

Chapter 18

Spelling

Eight more years went by. Harvey was staring at the sky. Distant cloudbanks beyond the horizon looked like vast continents spread across a planet much larger than Earth. He could see what looked like oceans and bays, sprawling river deltas, looming mountain ranges with their own even more distant layers of cloud. The voice was gone again, perhaps forever, but he didn't miss it anymore. Not really.

"One more thing," said the voice.

Harvey's heart jumped. He was always taken aback by the realization that the voice could startle him. A voice in your head should not be able to do that. He looked around the solarium, but the handful of oldsters were lost in their own thoughts.

"Oh, you're still here," he said, out loud, to the sky.

"Where did you think I was?"

"I thought you'd gone," said Harvey.

"Gone? Fat chance," said the voice. "I don't come and go. Thought you knew that by now."

"Well, gone from my immediate vicinity," Harvey ventured.

"Vicinity? My dear boy, we've been through all this, haven't we?"

Harvey felt the old annoyance rising again. *Dear boy?* Then he realized it no longer mattered. Nothing much mattered, really.

"I have been thinking about what you said last time," Harvey said.

"That's reassuring," said the voice.

"You said you would explain what life is."

"That's a tall order," said the voice.

"Yes, but you promised. If you're going to explain anything, now might be your last chance."

"We'll have plenty more chances."

"Maybe so. But are you going to explain anything or not?"

"Sometimes a thing has to be shown, rather than explained."

"But why?" said Harvey.

"Some things can't be explained."

"Things that can't be explained can still be understood? That sounds like a contradiction."

"It would be, if understanding meant being able to explain something. But some things can only be understood intuitively. Some things have to be understood in the heart, without words."

Harvey thought about that for a minute.

The voice went on. "Now look."

"Where?" said Harvey, and then in his mind he saw a glimpse of the rules. There were only eighteen of them, but they seemed so clear. Then he realized they weren't in words. They were just the knowledge of the rules.

He looked out at the solarium with its army of armchairs, but he could still see the rules, like a high-resolution image overlaid on everything around him. The rules had a kind of texture, and he looked closer at them and saw rules within rules covering everything in sight.

The distant sun-drenched mountains were covered with layers of rules. It was as if every detail of every object he could see had its own fine texture, and even the texture itself had a texture, and under each fine point of texture was another rule.

Rules governed every aspect of everything, layer upon layer of intelligence reaching down beyond his field of view, reaching out beyond his field of view.

"It's all rules," he said.

"Yes, that's the point," said the voice.

"That there are rules for everything?"

"No, that rules are a kind of intelligence, and everything's a manifestation of intelligence. Intelligence of the universe. Intelligence of the atom. Intelligence of the galaxy. Intelligence of empty space."

Harvey stared for a while. Seeing his inside understanding projected on the outside world was fascinating.

"The rules that we've been talking about," said the voice, "are rules for an individual person, how he interacts with all the other rules."

"But doesn't this still mean that everything is predefined? Predestined? Where's free will if everything is operating according to rules?"

"Don't be silly. There's plenty of room for free will," said the voice. "You've been using it all your life. Why question it now?"

"But these infinite rules contradict the idea of personal freedom or responsibility, don't they? The whole thing is just a giant mechanism."

"You can look at it that way," said the voice, "but I don't recommend it. As a mechanism, the complexity is so idiotically vast that it hardly matters!"

"Too vast to understand?"

"Too vast to explain."

"Oh."

"Too vast for words. But even in the purely mechanical view there's still room for many levels of freedom, many meanings of freedom."

"So what's the other view?"

"That the rules are just intelligence, rules at every level. So life is really just ripples of intelligence, energy obeying rules. Then you might glimpse something about the origin of that intelligence."

"You mean you?" said Harvey. "Are you the intelligence?"

"We're the intelligence," said the voice. "You and me."

"But that's preposterous," said Harvey.

"Isn't it?" said the voice. Bells again, louder than usual.

"Now you're really not making sense," said Harvey.

"I don't need to. It's all intelligence, the movement of knowledge. This raw, primordial intelligence is what you're physically made of. Everything is. No exceptions."

The voice fell silent for a while. Then it said, "Movement of knowledge. It moves by itself."

"I guess this makes sense to you, but not to me."

"But you are me. Rule 6b, remember?"

"Well," said Harvey, "I don't know the whole universe. If you *are* God, I've never had any way of validating that. And I definitely can't say that I know anything a god would know. It seems pretty obvious I'm not God."

"Correct," said the voice. "It's obvious. But what's obvious isn't always correct."

"Arg," groaned Harvey. "Word games." He sighed. "Why does it always come down to word games?"

"They're not word games, Harvey," said the voice. "They're word failures."

"Failures?"

"Words fail. The mind fails. The Game of Life is not a concept. It's not an idea. It can't be contained within the mind as a thought."

"And yet we're talking about it," said Harvey.

"But your mind is only a part of you, and you're only a part of the game. How can a part of a part contain the whole thing? How can words even do justice to the speaker of the words? Words aren't all-powerful. There are endless things they can't describe."

"Oh, I don't know," objected Harvey. "Words do pretty damn well most of the time."

"Do they? What does an orange taste like?"

Harvey's brain screeched to a stop. "Well, I ..."

"Explain how to tie a shoelace."

"Well, you ..." Harvey began. Then he said, "Yeah, I see what you mean. But with poetry, art ..."

"You're right," said the voice. "You can create an infinity of beautiful expressions with words, to be sure. But the infinity of things words *can't* describe is far, far greater."

"Different size infinities?"

"Absolutely. A basic idea, actually, if you think about it."

"I don't see that at all," said Harvey.

"Well, you'd need to know some math," said the voice.

"I was afraid of that," said Harvey. "Let's not go there, OK?"

"OK," said the voice, and then went there. "You can think of math as a kind of perfect language, since it doesn't have to describe anything real, or physical. It's beyond what's known by the senses, which are limited and distorted."

"So?"

"Even though it's pure, math has shown that even the reasoning that underlies words has to be limited. No matter how well you design the language."

"Why are you telling me this?"

"Just to make a point: Descriptions, no matter how accurate, are never complete."

"OK. I'll buy that."

"So don't let it bother you that you can't always get a decent explanation of everything that really matters."

Harvey was silent for a while. "Then what's the point of saying anything? About stuff that matters?"

"Because even if you can't describe the taste of an orange, you can still point at one."

Harvey was tired when the conversation started, and now he was close to his limit. "I'm still not God," he said.

"You're completely convinced that you're not me, aren't you?"

"'Fraid so," said Harvey.

"Well," said the voice, "You not being God doesn't mean I can't enjoy being you."

"You never got around to today's rule," said Harvey. "What is it? I'm getting really tired."

"I thought you'd never ask," said the voice. "Rule 18: ***Spelling counts.***"

"Good lord," said Harvey.

"Yup."

"I meant the rule."

"I know. It's more important than it sounds."

"That's hard to believe."

"Don't overlook the little things."

"Like spelling?"

"You won't allow me a little poetic license?"

"Fine. I've got to dot my 't's and cross my 'i's."

"There's more to it than that."

"Oh?"

"Everything counts."

"Oh dear."

"It's not a warning, you know. Just an observation about how it works."

"I know. I guess."

Harvey sat back and gazed out the window at the mountains for a while. His eyelids were getting heavy. He could hear some bluejays screeching outside the center.

"This latest rule," said the voice.

"Yes? What about it."

"Don't you forget it."

"You can't be serious."

"I never am." The voice paused for a long time. "And neither should you," it said.

Ω

Epilogue

It was some time later, days or weeks, maybe even years. Harvey was always tired now, but inside he was inexplicably elated. *So I guess this whole thing was just the process of learning the rules,* he thought. *Seems kind of strange that the game itself is just learning the rules.*

And then he thought, *Maybe it wasn't the rules at all. I didn't really put them to much use. Maybe it was the voice.* The only common thread he could find was his relationship with the voice. Or with himself. *Maybe that's what it was all about.* He had always wondered if he wasn't just talking to himself all along.

He looked out the window by his bed, but it was all sky. He couldn't see the lake without sitting up, if there was a lake. Was there a lake? He wasn't sure any more, but he could hear the afternoon whitecaps against the rocks. It hadn't been a bad run at all. A lot of water under the bridge, but the pine tree in upstate New York didn't seem all that far away. *It really wasn't about the rules, or all those incidents they might have applied to,* he thought. *It was just about that dialog, wasn't it?*

"Talking to yourself again?" said the voice. "Now we're getting somewhere."

. . .

Sleep came for a few hours, and went away briefly, and then returned. The afternoon sky grew dark, and the traffic sounds outside increased as people began driving home for dinner. A horn sounded outside the center. Harvey opened his eyes.

We could be friends, couldn't we? thought Harvey. Then he added, "I guess we already are ... don't you think?"

Bells.

Ω

www.ingramcontent.com/pod-product-compliance
Lightning Source LLC
Chambersburg PA
CBHW030530020726
47494CB00004B/1291